Grimey Ways

Ray Vinci

**Lock Down Publications and Ca$h
Presents**

Grimey Ways

A Novel by *Ray Vinci*

Grimey Ways

Lock Down Publications
P.O. Box 944
Stockbridge, Ga 30281

Visit our website @
www.lockdownpublications.com

Copyright 2021 by Ray Vinci
Grimey Ways

First Edition December 2021
Printed in the United States of America

This is a work of fiction. Names, characters, places, and incidents either are products of the author's imagination or are used fictitiously. Any similarity to actual events or locales or persons, living or dead, is entirely coincidental.

Lock Down Publications
Like our page on Facebook: Lock Down Publications @
www.facebook.com/lockdownpublications.ldp

Book interior design by: **Shawn Walker**
Edited by: **Jill Alicea**

Ray Vinci

Stay Connected with Us!

Text **LOCKDOWN** to 22828 to stay up-to-date with new re-
leases, sneak peaks, contests and more…
Thank you.

Submission Guideline

Submit the first three chapters of your completed manuscript to <u>ldpsubmissions@gmail.com</u>, subject line: Your book's title. The manuscript must be in a .doc file and sent as an attachment. Document should be in Times New Roman, double spaced and in size 12 font. Also, provide your synopsis and full contact information. If sending multiple submissions, they must each be in a separate email.

Have a story but no way to send it electronically? You can still submit to LDP/Ca$h Presents. Send in the first three chapters, written or typed, of your completed manuscript to:

LDP: Submissions Dept
Po Box 944
Stockbridge, Ga 30281

DO NOT send original manuscript. Must be a duplicate.

Provide your synopsis and a cover letter containing your full contact information.

Thanks for considering LDP and Ca$h Presents.

Ray Vinci

Chapter 1

It'd been six months since Kilo had been home, and he was back to doing the same shit he was doing that got him locked up. All he thought about was getting money and robbing and killing was the only way he knew how to get it. Before he went down, he put together a team of six called the Stick-up Squad. If you was getting it, they were sticking you for it, plain and simple.

Niggas feared the Stick-up Squad. When they were around, muthafuckas tucked their chains and hid their cash. The Squad ran shit and it wasn't shit they couldn't have.

Kilo was woken out of his sleep to banging on his door. He slid out of bed angry as fuck and talking shit, because there was no way niggas should be knocking on his door that early in the morning.

"Who the fuck is it?" he yelled, cursing at whoever it was at his door.

"It's Illy. Open the door before I kick this bitch down. We got shit to talk about!"

Illy was his li'l brother and also second in command of the Stick-up Squad. Although Illy was his li'l bro, he was bigger than him all around. He was 6'2" and weighed 200 pounds. Every time you saw him, he was in the flyest shit and stayed strapped up.

"Damn, nigga, you gon' sleep all day or get this money?" Illy asked.

"Shit, the only thing to do is get money," he said, giving his li'l bro dap and at the same time using the line they used to say growing up. "Talk to me, gangsta, what's on ya mind?" Kilo asked.

"We been checking out this nigga named Rico for a while, and the nigga getting paper like it ain't shit," Illy said. "Word on the street is the nigga capping and saying he can't be touched."

"Then why the fuck we ain't hit his spot yet?" Kilo asked with an attitude.

"Well, Babygurl been getting close to the nigga. She been to all his spots, and she got it set up to where it goes down tonight," said Illy.

Babygurl was someone you couldn't resist no matter how hard you tried. Babygurl was a bad Mexican bitch with long straight hair that went to the middle of her back. At 5'2" and 135 pounds, Babygurl was stacked with titties and ass. Most people thought she was a Mexican trapped in a black girl's body. She was about her money.

"Alright, let me get myself together and we'll meet up at the spot so we can go over everything."

"Bet. Hit me up when you ready," Illy said as he was walking out of the door. "You know Babygurl still got love for you."

"Yeah, I know. It's always been like that since day one. Now get the fuck out of my shit." He pushed him out the door.

As he was getting ready, he couldn't help but think about Babygurl and what Illy said before he left. He and Babygurl had been fucking around since they were thirteen and now at nineteen, the love was still there. Since day one, she'd been holding him down. Even when he was locked up Babygurl held him down with letters, money, phone calls, and visits. The last few months he heard nothing from her. Word on the streets was she was with somebody else and was done with him.

Grimey Ways

***

As soon as he stepped outside, he heard his name being called.

"Kilo, Kilo! Damn, you don't fuck with me no more or what?" Lexi said with a smile on her face. Lexi was a sight to see. At 5'4" and 120 pounds, she was banging. For her to be that size, Lexi had ass out of this world. Lexi was half-black and half-Mexican with long curly hair, caramel skin, and a beautiful smile.

"What's up, half-breed? You know we tight. I just been busy lately," said Kilo.

"Already? What you looking all fly for? Where you going?" she asked, eyeing him from head to toe.

Kilo was 6'0" and weighed 185 pounds. His hair was always cut to a low taper with waves all around. Kilo was always fly no matter what he was in. He had on some grey 501 pants with a black T-shirt and some black Air Force Ones. He was a dark-skinned nigga that everybody loved.

"I got some business to handle later. Why, what you got going on?" Kilo asked, smiling from ear to ear.

"Nothing. I'm tryna kick it wit' you for a li'l while."

"Well, let's go get something to eat. I'm hungry as hell."

"Okay." She followed him towards his truck.

They jumped in his truck and drove down Martin Luther King. On the way to get something to eat, they got to know each other better. They pulled up to Baysea's off W.W. White and walked in.

"You think you fly in that truck, don't you?" Lexi asked while stuffing fish in her mouth.

"Naw. Just had to treat myself to something since I been home."

"What did you do time for, if you don't mind me asking?"

"Aggravated robbery with a deadly weapon." He looked up to see her facial expression. "I hope I didn't scare you."

"What? I likes me a gangsta nigga." Before she could finish her sentence, she was looking at her phone. "That was my sister. I'm supposed to meet up and chill with her today," she said with an attitude. "Can you drop me off on the northeast side, please?"

"Yeah. I gotta meet up with my squad anyways."

On the way to the northeast side, it was quiet, so all he could think about was how life could be with Lexi. She was the type he could chill with - no drama, no nothing, just him and her. He pulled up on Spring Hill off Raybon and parked.

"Well, thank you for taking me out to lunch. I really enjoyed it," she said.

"You welcome. We can do it again sometime, if it's cool with you."

"Nigga, what took you so long to ask anyways?" Lexi asked while punching him on his shoulder.

"Look, take my number and hit me up."

She took it and jumped out of the truck. He sat there until somebody let her in. She looked back at him and smiled while blowing him a kiss.

Chapter 2

"Damn, where the fuck this nigga at? I been waiting on this nigga for damn near five hours."

Correy was 5'9" and weighed 190 pounds. Every time you saw him he had a fade, cargo shorts, and a white T-shirt.

"Sit down, the nigga gon' come. Shit, you know he take his time every time you call," Lovey said with irritation in her voice.

"I know. I just 'on't trust these San Antonio niggas like that, Joe."

"Ain't shit gon' happen to you. Niggas ain't worried about you. You been nervous since you came from Chicago."

While Lovey was talking, somebody knocked on the door. Correy jumped up and ran to the door with his banger.

"Who is it? Correy asked whoever was on the other side of the door.

"It's Lexi. Let me in. It's hot as hell out here!"

Correy opened the door while Lexi was waving and blowing a kiss to whoever was in the truck.

"What's up, Correy? Why you always answer the door with that gun in yo' hand, with yo' scary ass?" Lexi said, laughing at Correy.

"'Cause I can. And who the hell is that you got dropping you off at my shit?"

"None of yo' business. Where Lovey at anyways?" Lexi asked as soon as Lovey came from the backroom.

Lovey looked just like Lexi, but thicker and darker. Lovey was two years younger than Lexi and one year older than Lisa, who looked exactly like them.

"What's up, sis? What took you so long to get here?" asked Lovey.

"I went out with Kilo, with his sexy ass," Lexi said, sounding happy.

"You still tryna get with that nigga?" she said while they sat down on the couch. "The nigga my age, but anyways..."

"So? I'm twenty-one, he nineteen. Mind yo' business," she said while rolling her eyes at Lovey. "Damn, y'all shit decked out."

Correy and Lovey's two-bedroom apartment had flat screens in every room, brown leather couches to match their their curtains, and carpet, pictures of African people hanging on the wall, and a bad-ass bedroom and kitchen set.

A car horn sounded from outside. Correy rushed to the window to see who it was.

"'Bout gotdamn time! Shit! I'm missing all kinds of money waiting on this nigga," he said, rushing out the door. Correy jumped in Philly's navy-blue BMW and started talking shit.

"Damn, Joe, what took you so long?"

"Nigga, I told you I was coming and you blowing my phone up and shit. What you need so I can bounce?" Philly shot back.

"Give me a brick. I got $25,000, Joe. When you gon' look out for me? It's too much money out here for just one brick."

"I don't trust niggas out here, but if you come out wit' $100,000, I can give you five of 'em. That's five off of each one."

"Bet. Let me go whip this up and I'ma get back at you."

"I'ma slide through tonight and pick you up so we can hit the studio and drop some tracks," Philly said, then smashed off.

12

It took Correy a couple of hours to do what he had to do. While he was cooking up the bricks, he was thinking of all kind of ways to get money. Spring Hill was a gold mine. You had niggas that was buying it to sell, and niggas copping it to smoke. If he had a team he could trust, he could take over, but until he found one, fuck it, it was get rich and fuck everybody else.

His thoughts were interrupted by Lovey calling his name

"Damn, nigga, you can't be into cooking that shit like that. My sister wanna know if you can take her back home?" Lovey said, annoyed at Correy and rolling her eyes.

"Yeah, but she gotta roll with us to make a couple of dollars 'cause I got people waiting on me."

"Alright, let us know when you ready," she said as she walked out of the kitchen.

When Correy was done in the kitchen, he walked into the living room and saw Lovey and Lexi in deep conversation and passing a Sweet.

"Let me hit that loud," Correy said while reaching for the Sweet. "What's up, y'all ready to bounce or what?"

"Yeah and give me my shit before you smoke it all." She snatched her blunt, then she walked to the car.

Correy had a Chevy Yukon sitting on 30" rims, black-on-black with a mean-ass system in the back. When he got in the truck, Lovey and Lexi were already finished with the blunt.

"Damn, y'all finished that loud pack? Y'all stingy," he said with a fucked-up look on his face.

All they could do could do was laugh because they were high as fuck.

Correy jumped on I-35 and headed to Fredrickberg Road. When he got to Woodlawn Apartments, niggas ran up to his truck like he was a superstar.

"Where the fuck you been? I been missing sales all day waiting on you to come through!" One nigga came with an attitude.

"You betta watch who the fuck you talking to like that before I won't serve yo' ass shit!" Correy said, making sure his point was clear.

He made a couple more stops that way, then got back on the freeway to take Lexi home.

"What you got going on later on tonight?" Lovey asked her sister. "I'm tryna go to Joe's since he going to the studio,"

"I can go with you. I ain't shit else to do," Lexi said.

"Alright. I'ma hit you up wheneva I'm ready, Okay?"

"Bye, girl," she said while getting out of the truck.

Correy drove all around San Antonio making money. He remembered when his momma first told him he was moving to Texas. At first he was fucked up about leaving Chicago and his homies. He felt like he was being disloyal to his friends by leaving. He had gotten into some shit with some niggas and the beef got too out of hand, so his momma told him he had to move to Texas so he could start over.

When he got to San Antonio, he had no source of income, so he had to do what he did best. After a year, he hooked up with Philly. Philly saw that he was hungry and gave him some work. Now he had his own place, car, and money.

Correy jumped at the sound of his phone and answered it quickly. His phone was worth a million dollars on any given Sunday.

"What's up? Talk to me," said Correy.

"Say, homie, I need five of them thangs. What's it gon' run me?" said Rico.

"It's gon' run you $125,000 but let me hit my nigga up so I can get it," he said, then hung up. Correy knew what he could do with $25,000. It seemed liked the money kept coming his way, so he kept stacking.

"My nigga say it's good. Meet me on Fredrickberg at the trap. I got you!" he told Rico and then hung up.

Ray Vinci

Chapter 3

Kilo drove down Martin Luther King, listening to the new Lil Baby album while on his way to Skinnie's block to meet up with his squad. They had just called him up and told him that Babygurl just saw Rico cop five bricks and they were on their way to the Rivceras off of Peacan Valley. When he got there, he saw his squad posted up at the Phillip 66.

Illy, Low-Key, Felony, and Slugga were all happy to see him when he jumped out of his truck.

"What's up with this clown-ass nigga Rico?" Kilo asked while greeting his squad.

"Shit, we waiting on Babygurl to hit us back up," Low-key said.

Low-key had grown up with Kilo and Illy. He was also Babygurl's cousin. Low-key was a mixed breed but looked more like he was just a light-skinned nigga. He was 5'11" and 195 pounds of pure muscle. Every time he came around, he had a different bitch.

"Well, let's make our way to the south eastside so we can be ready," Illy said.

When they got to the Rivceras, Babygurl texted Illy and told him what apartment they were in.

***

Babygurl was sitting in the living room next to Rico, just chilling. Rico's shit was fly. He had a 72"-inch flat screen TV with surround sound and a mean-ass stereo system hooked up to it. He had an X-box One with every game you could think

17

of. He had suede couches with recliners on each end and white curtains to match his carpets.

"Roll that drink up while I go take a piss."

Rico thought he was fly. He had good wavy hair and a deep voice that the ladies loved. He was 6'4", light-skinned with buck teeth, and all he wore was Nike, T-shirts and Trues. While Rico went to take a piss, Babygurl unlocked the door and let the squad in.

"Where that bitch-ass nigga at?" Kilo asked Babygurl while handing her a black 9mm.

"He in the restroom——"

Before she could finish her sentence, she heard the bathroom door open. By the time Rico came around the corner, he had six barrels pointing at his face.

"Take one more step and I'll blow yo' fuckin brains all ova this playa-ass carpet you got!" Slugga said with a mug on his face.

"Bitch! You set me up. I knew you was a no-good bitch from the jump. All you had was some good pussy and a good head game anyway," Rico said calmly.

Before Rico could laugh, Kilo slapped the shit out of him with his 40 cal.

"You betta watch yo' fucking mouth, gangsta," said Kilo. "All you gotta do is give up what we want and we'll be out yo' shit."

"I don't have shit here. You at the wrong spot, playboy." Rico said with a mouth full of blood. *Damn, how did I get myself into some shit like this, fucking with this hoe and thinking with my dick!* he thought.

"Tie this nigga up. He gon' tell us one way or another," Kilo told Felony. "As a matter of fact, Illy, Low-Key, and Slugga, shake this bitch down while we handle this nigga."

Babygurl stepped in front of Rico and spit in his face. "I got something for yo' pussy ass for disrespecting a gangsta bitch," she said while cocking her 9mm.

Kilo and Felony gave each other a curious look, but before they could ask her what she was about to do, she shot him in each of his kneecaps.

"Ahhhh!" Rico screamed in pain.

"Now, I'm gon' ask you one more time: where is the money and the work? We know you just copped five bricks, gangsta," Kilo said, getting aggravated.

"Fuck you and them pussy-ass niggas you with."

Felony started pistol-whipping him until they couldn't recognize him anymore.

Before they could ask him again, Illy, Slugga, and Low-key came from the back with three black duffle bags.

"Looks like we was just in time. Where was you going, gangsta?" Kilo asked with a gun in his face. "Load up the truck. Me and Babygurl got this."

While the squad loaded up Kilo's truck, he and Babygurl wiped away any prints that they could have left.

"What you want me to do with this nigga, Kilo?" Babygurl asked.

"I don't care."

When Kilo said that Babygurl emptied the clip into Rico's face.

"Bitch-ass nigga."

They both walked out of the door like nothing had happened.

"You can ride with me, Babygurl," said Kilo.

When she got in the truck, he smiled as he looked at his gangsta bitch and drove off.

On the way to Kilo's spot, it was quiet except for the Moneybagg Yo playing. Kilo's eyes were on the road, but he still saw Babygurl looking at him like she wanted to say something. Kilo turned up the radio and remembered the first time Babygurl said she was his gangsta bitch.

"I'ma be yo' gangsta bitch til the end," she had said right when they got done pulling their first lick together.

Kilo was snapped back to reality when Babygurl turned the music down.

"What's up, nigga? You act like you don't see me!" Babygurl said, sounding like she was Mexican for the first time. She was hurt that Kilo hadn't spoken to her since he'd been out.

"Look, you stopped fucking with me at a time I needed you the most and now you wanna act like the shit ain't even happen," he said calmly while looking in her eyes and lighting a Newport.

"I needed to do what I had to do to set this lick up so when you got home you was good. Shit, I had to eat while you was locked up!" she yelled at Kilo while pointing her fingers in his face.

"You need to watch how the fuck you talking to me before I swell yo' lips shut! Ain't shit sweet!" he said, making sure his point was clear. "Shit changed for me and you. I got much love for you, but we done."

She looked at him with fear and hurt in her eyes because she knew where he was coming from. "I know, but I'm always gon' be yo' gangsta bitch, right?" she asked with a fake smile on her face. She knew she had hurt him but was going to do whatever she had to do to get him back.

"Of course, you gon' always be that nobody could never take that from you." He kissed her on her forehead then they got out of the truck and went in to count up the money.

It took them thirty minutes to count up everything and split it up. Altogether they had $90,000, five bricks, and two pounds of doe-doe, so everyone got $15,000 apiece.

"What y'all wanna do with these bricks?" Kilo asked the squad.

"Shit, you can keep that shit as a welcome home gift," said Babygurl.

"I say we smoke something," Slugga said.

"How about we celebrate?" Illy said.

"Hell yeah!"

"Alright, we got a couple of hours. Let's get ready and meet up at Joe's at 9:00 p.m.," Kilo said.

"Bet," added Felony.

***

"What's up, sis?" was all Lexi said when she picked up her phone.

"It's 7:00 p.m. You almost ready?" Lovey asked.

"Yeah, I'm finding something to wear right now. By the time you get here, I'ma be ready."

"I'ma be there in thirty minutes," she said and then hung up.

Lexi walked to her closet. It took her all of ten minutes to figure out what she was going to wear.

All Lexi could think about was looking good and being the baddest bitch in the club. Lexi checked her reflection in the mirror to see how she looked in her pink Louis Vuitton dress that went to her thighs and her pink pumps that wrapped around her calf. Her designer earrings, bracelet, and necklace stood out. She had decided to let her hair down and rock her curly hair.

Right when she finished getting ready, her sister pulled up and blew the horn. Lovey got out to give her sister a hug.

"Damn, bitch, what, you tryna have every nigga in the club on you tonight?" Lovey asked while looking her up and down.

"You ain't too bad yourself."

Lovey had on a black freak 'em dress that showed off every curve and some black pumps that looked similar to Lexi's. Lovey had her hair in a ponytail so she could show off her Chanel ear rings.

"Where the weed at? I know Correy left you some of that fire?"

"Best believe it. Come on before it get too packed and we can't get in," Lovey said as she jumped in her silver Altima.

Before they drove off, she popped in Nikki Minaj and headed to Joe's. On the way to Joe's, she thought about the last time she went to the club. Last time she had to leave early. This time she was going to have fun. When they pulled up to the parking lot, it was jumping.

"Damn, it's live out here in the parking lot, so I know the inside live," Lexi said, smiling from ear to ear.

Chapter 4

Kilo and the squad were in the back posted up in VIP. They figured fuck it, let's do it big. They had Ciroc and Grey Goose bottles everywhere while they toasted to a job well done. It seemed like every female was trying to push their way into VIP. Some got in and some didn't make it because Babygurl started checking shit. Kilo sat back watching everything moving. Kilo always watched everything. He was always looking out for the lick and the next fuck. Tonight, he was looking out for whoever was talking about what happened to Rico.

"Man, them gots to be two of the baddest bitches in the club," Low-key said to Kilo.

"Nigga, I ain't worried about no bitches. I'm chilling, tryna see what's shakin'."

"I'm 'bout to go see what's up with 'em' and bring them back," Low-key said, walking towards the bar.

When Kilo looked up to see where Low-key was headed, he saw who Low-key was talking about. Kilo was mesmerized by Lexi and couldn't stop staring at her. Before he could tell his crew were he was going, he took off towards the bar.

On the way to the bar, niggas that knew Kilo gave him daps and bitches gave him hugs. Kilo hardly paid any attention to who they were because he was stuck on Lexi. By the time he got to the bar, Low-Key was already chopping it up with Lovey.

"Superstars belong in VIP," Kilo said, walking up behind Lexi.

Lexi turned around to see who was talking to her and a smile appeared on her face when she saw that it was Kilo. *Damn this nigga fine as hell*, Lexi thought.

"Hey Kilo, what you doing up in here?" she asked.

"Shit, celebrating a job well done. What you doing up here?" asked Kilo.

"I'm here with my sister Lovey. You looking good. What you do, hit the lotto?" He had on some black Polo jeans and a gray and white Polo shirt with the Polo horse from the top to the bottom. He also had on some gray and white Retro 11s and a black and silver San Antonio Spurs snapback.

"Naw, no lotto, but you not looking too bad yourself. Turn around and let me look at you, sexy," Kilo said, admiring every curve on her body.

Lexi knew she was looking good so she turned around so Kilo wouldn't miss anything.

"I see the homie got yo' sister jammed up over there. Let's go to VIP. Me and my squad got it for the night."

"Okay, let me get my sister."

***

"Who is that bitch Kilo over there talking to?" Babygurl asked Illy while staring at the bar.

"I don't know. Stop worrying about that nigga. All these niggas in the club and you stunnin' him." Illy was getting annoyed at Babygurl because all she was talking about was Kilo. Illy had watched Babygurl and Kilo go through so much shit, and he hated to see her hurt. When Illy looked up and saw Low-key and his brother with two of the baddest bitches in the club, he saw why Babygurl was mad.

"What's up, big bro? Who this y'all got with y'all?" Illy asked, looking at both Lexi and Lovey.

"Lexi and Lovey, this is my li'l bro Illy, Babygurl, Felony, and Slugga," Kilo said, introducing them to the Squad.

24

Lexi noticed Babygurl giving her a fucked-up look, but she brushed it off.

"Hey. How y'all doing?" Lexi said while sitting next to Kilo.

Kilo and Lexi were all up in each other's ears. They were doing everything: kissing, touching, and hugging. They might as well have been fucking. Babygurl was watching them the whole time and she didn't like what she was seeing. Babygurl stood up, contemplating if she wanted to stomp her and her sister, but thought twice.

"Look out, Low key. I'ma go to the bar for a li'l while. Roll with me," Babygurl told Low-key while walking away.

Kilo knew Babygurl was fucked up about what was going on, but right now he was feeling Lexi.

Low-key took off after Babygurl because he knew why she left. When he caught up to Babygurl, she was yanking her arm away from some nigga. The nigga didn't like what she did and yanked it back. Low-key eased up on him.

"Say, homie, watch who you grabbin' on before we touch everything in this bitch," he said, ready to jump shit off.

"Mind yo' fuckin' business, gangsta. This ain't got shit to do with you."

Low-key hit the nigga with a right hook that stumbled him into the bar. Low-key slid up on him and threw two quick punches that landed right on homeboy's chin. The punches seemed like they didn't even faze him because he shook it off and hit Low-key with a hard upper cut.

The nigga ran up on Low-key, grabbed him, and then slung him to the ground. Low-key was on point and jumped up as quickly as possible. He posted up, waiting on him to run up on him. Just like he was expecting, the nigga did it, and

25

Low-key side-stepped him then threw a three-piece combo that dropped him.

When the squad finally realized what was going on, Kilo was already making his way through the crowd. Right when he got in sight, he noticed the nigga pull a knife. Before the nigga made it to Low-key, Kilo was up on him with the 40 cal. to his side.

"Take one more step and it will be ya last one, homie," Kilo whispered in his ear.

"Naw, it ain't even like that, gangsta."

"Well, you need to get the fuck out this bitch before we leave it a crime scene," said Kilo.

Babygurl was at his side, trying to calm him down before it got of hand. "Chill, here comes security. Put that gun away." said Babygurl.

"Y'all good this way?" the security guard said.

"Yeah, we straight we about to dip right now." Kilo told him. Kilo and the squad walked back to VIP where they had left Lexi and Lovey.

"What happened over there, and why you looking pissed off?" Lovey asked Low-key.

"I just smashed on some nigga for touching my cousin," said Low-key.

"Come on, let's dip before the nigga come back trippin'," said Kilo.

As they made it through the crowd, trying to get to the door, he heard some niggas talking. It seemed the whole squad heard them and they all pulled their burners.

"Say, I'ma get up wit' y'all later. Go home with your sister," Kilo told Lexi.

As soon as Lexi walked off to the car with Lovey, they heard tires screeching from down the street. When Kilo turned around, he saw a black-on-black Cadillac speeding towards them with the windows down. He saw someone hanging out of the window. He grabbed Babygurl and dove to the ground. By that time, shots were already ringing out.

Choppa bullets were flying everywhere as the crowd was running and screaming, trying to get out of the way. When the car was gon', Illy was the only one that stood up.

"Everybody good?" he asked his squad.

"Yeah." It seemed that everybody said it all at once.

Once everybody was off of the ground, the Cadillac hit the block again, but before it could let off some shots, the whole squad was letting loose on the car. The squad didn't let up until the Caddy started swerving and crash into a pole. Before anybody could say something, Kilo and Illy ran up on the car and emptied the rest of their clips to make sure nobody was left alive.

When Kilo and Illy met up with the squad outside of the club, they heard police sirens.

"Let's dip. The laws are on the way," Felony said.

"Kilo, can you drop me off? I rode with my cousin," Babygurl asked Kilo.

"Yeah," he said. They both hopped in the truck and then smashed off.

"You Okay? You not hurt or nothing?" she asked Kilo with concern.

"Yeah, I'm good. Where am I taking you?"

"I don't wanna go to Low-key's spot. Can I chill with you?"

"I knew you was on some slick shit," said Kilo.

Babygurl was the type that always had to have her way. She knew that staying with Kilo, he wouldn't be able to resist her. Kilo was her world. They had been through so much shit.

Kilo was the only nigga she had actually been with besides Rico, and Rico was only because she had to.

Babygurl could tell he was feeling Lexi by the way he was up on her in the club. They both had her fucked up if they thought she wasn't going to do anything about it.

"So, you and ole girl getting pretty close, huh?" she asked Kilo

"Yeah, something like that. She cool."

"I hope you happy with her because she seems happy with you."

"What's up wit' all this happy shit? We just got shot at and you talking about this shit," he said, looking at her.

She said nothing because she felt hurt by what Kilo had going on with Lexi.

For the rest of the ride, it was quiet. When Kilo pulled up to his house, his phone started ringing. He looked at the caller ID and saw that it was Lexi. He started to answer, but didn't, because he knew Babygurl would start tripping. He put the phone on vibrate, then shoved it back in its pocket.

When they walked in, Kilo went straight to the living room. He had a nice laid-back apartment. His furniture was black suede along with the rest of the living room. His room was like his man cave. His king-sized bed was dressed in black sheets along with a thick grey blanket with pillowcases that matched his sheets. His curtain were black with designs up and down them, plus the flat screen and PS4 to entertain him.

"I got some dank on the table. Roll something up while I take a shower," Kilo said walking to towards the back. "I got some extra shit in the room if you wanna get comfortable."

It took him fifteen minutes to shower and when he walked out of the bathroom in just his boxers, Babygurl went crazy.

Damn, this nigga been working out. He sexy as hell. "You had to come in here with just yo' boxers on," she said, eyeing his whole body.

"You act like you ain't never seen this shit before. Light the Sweet."

He sat on the couch next to Babygurl and smoked doe-doe for an hour. Out of nowhere, Babygurl reached over and grabbed his dick. Kilo jumped because he was surprised by what she did. He was going to say no, but he was horny as fuck. He hadn't had any pussy since he'd been home and was feeling the weed. When she pulled his dick out of his boxers, her eyes almost popped out of her head.

"Damn, this bitch done got big as fuck."

Before he could say anything, she stuck his dick in her mouth and went all the way down in one motion. When she came back up, she went right back down without even taking a breath. She used so much spit that his balls were soaking wet. She made all kinds of slurping noises as she tried to give him the best dick sucking of his life. Kilo had almost forgotten how good Babygurl's head game was and he almost busted a nut.

Kilo grabbed her, then flipped her on her back. He pulled her shirt over her head and to his surprise, that was all she had on. He started sucking on her titties like there was no tomorrow.

"Hurry up and fuck me," she moaned.

He put her legs over his shoulders and entered her slowly.

"Uh! Daddy, I missed this dick," she managed to say between strokes.

Before she knew it, Kilo plowed down into her, putting all 8 ½ inches of his dick inside her. Her insides were already hurting and he'd just gotten started.

Damn, this nigga got some good dick, she couldn't help but think.

"Act like this pussy is yours, daddy. Fuck me!" She was in ecstasy because she hadn't been fucked like that in so long. She wanted Kilo to feel all of her, so she spread her legs as wide as she could. As soon as she did that, she regretted it. It felt like Kilo was in her stomach.

He turned her around and entered her from the back, He went crazy when he saw the waves he was making her ass do every time he hit it.

She met him thrust for thrust and threw it back at him with every stroke he gave. She pulled away and pushed him on his back, then straddled him. She sat all the way down on him, making his whole dick disappear in her wet pussy. She moved slowly, making sure he felt every wall she had. She grinded, bounced, and wiggled on his dick. She had cum twice already and could feel the third one on its way.

"I'm cumming, daddy! Uhhhh!" she screamed, releasing cum on his dick for the third time.

Kilo was so turned on by her wet pussy and feeling her cum that he came right behind her. She knew he was cumming because he grew an extra inch inside of her. She collapsed on his chest and they both lay there until they fell asleep.

Chapter 5

When she opened her eyes, she almost forgot where she was. Lexi set up on the couch, remembering everything that happened last night.

She didn't know what everything was about, but her only concern was Kilo. She was getting too close to Kilo and was falling in love with him. She knew what she was getting herself into so her mind was telling her no, but her heart was overpowering her mind.

Last night she remembered texting the Kilo to see if he was Okay, but she didn't get an answer. She knew he was capable of taking care of himself, but she was still worried. Lexi's thoughts were interrupted when Lovey came from the back room.

"What up, girl? Last night was crazy. Have you heard from Kilo?" Lovey asked.

"No. I tried to text him but he didn't answer," Lexi said, trying to hide the concern in her voice.

Lovey walked over to the couch and at the same time reached for the remote to turn the TV on.

"Put it on the news to see if that shit that Kilo got into made it," Lexi said.

Lovey put it on KSAT-12. It was already on breaking news, and the reporter was talking about what went down at the club.

"Last night at Club Joe's Volcano, four people were murdered in what seemed like an all-out shootout. Witnesses say it began in a brawl inside of the club, and next thing they knew, bullets were flying everywhere. Neither victims nor suspects have been identified at this moment, so we're asking that anybody knows anything about these people that they please come forward."

In seconds, Lexi had her phone in her hand, trying to get in contact with Kilo. When he didn't answer his phone, she just knew something was wrong.

"Don't worry; he's alright. He's probably just laying low. I'll tell Correy to ride by his spot later on," Lovey said when she saw Lexi's eyes get watery.

Lovey knew her sister was in love once she saw her sister start crying. Lovey snapped her head from Lexi to the TV once she heard what the reporter was saying.

"Early yesterday around 12:00 p.m. it was reported that Ricardo Johnson a.k.a. Rico on the streets, was found dead in his apartment. Rico had been beaten badly and he had gunshot wounds to each of his knees and multiple shots to his face. When police entered his home, it was ransacked. If there are any witnesses or anybody with information, please come forward to help police solve this matter."

"Correy!" Lovey yelled.

"What the fuck is ya yelling for?" Correy asked while catching the end of the news clip.

"Rico dead. He got robbed and killed right after we left him," she said, looking back at Correy. She saw the hurt in his eyes. She knew Rico was like a brother to him. Correy just sat next to Lovey and lit up a Newport to let it sit on his brain.

"Somebody got to die! I don't give a fuck who it is! But somebody gots to die!" Correy said while slamming his fist down on the coffee table as hard as he could.

He sat there quietly while finishing his Newport. He was thinking about the last time he saw Rico. He knew something just didn't sit right, and he was gonna start with the Mexican broad Rico was with.

***

Kilo had just jumped out of the shower when he decided to turn his phone back on. When he turned his phone back on, he had a bunch of missed calls and messages from Lexi and his squad. He started to hit Lexi up, but he decided not to. He was feeling Lexi and knew he fucked up by doing what he did with Babygurl last night.

Kilo put on some gray and white Jordan basketball shorts and his all-white Air Max 90's. He figured he didn't need no shirt since he was just chilling at the crib today.

He grabbed a Dutch Master and some doe-doe. Right after that, he texted Lexi and told her to come kick it for a while at the crib. Lexi had texted him back and told him she was already on her way and that her sister and her nigga were coming too.

Kilo walked outside to his truck and turned up the Moneybagg Yo that was already in his deck from last night.

Right when he lit up his blunt of doe-doe, he saw a black Yukon pull up. Due to being paranoid from last night, he reached under his seat and grabbed his 40 cal. When he looked up and saw Lexi running towards him, he felt an instant relief. She was so happy to see him that she jumped into his arms and started kissing him everywhere she could.

"Damn, you had me a bit worried about you. I thought something happened to you," Lexi said, punching him in the chest.

"Naw, I'm good," he said, smiling.

"Put that big-ass gun away and let me hit that weed," she said. "Come meet my sister's boyfriend."

Lexi had already taken off while he was tucking his heat back under the seat. By the time he made it to the truck, Lovey was already pulling on his Sweet.

"What's good, Lovey, how are you doing?"

"I'm cool. Are you alright?" she asked

"Yeah, I'm good. You gon' introduce me or what?"

"What up, Joe? I'm Correy," Correy said, looking him up and down.

"Kilo." He gave him a stupid look. There was something about that nigga that he didn't like.

Lexi saw the way Kilo was mugging Correy so she tapped him and passed him the Sweet back.

"Say, Lexi, we gotta bounce. I gotta get this money. What you gonna do?" Correy asked Lexi.

"I got her. She gon' kick it with me today," Kilo said to Correy because he felt the tension.

"Alright, sis, hit me up later on," Lovey said as they pulled off.

Kilo locked up his truck, then he and Lexi went inside.

"What was all that about with you and Correy?" she said while sitting down on the bed.

"Shit, the nigga was plexed up with me so I plexed back. It's something about the nigga I don't like."

"Well, his homeboy just got killed, so you have to excuse his attitude," she said. "Damn, this bed soft." She lay down and Kilo lay next to her, then kissed her soft on the lips.

"We can put some dents in it if you want to," he said while smiling.

"I'm pretty sure we can with all this you got right here," she said while grabbing his dick. "That might be too much dick to take."

"It might be, but that's gon' have to wait because I'm taking you shopping. These ain't gonna do."

"I know you ain't cappin'?"

Kilo got up, put on a shirt and grabbed his hat, and some more weed. They jumped in his truck and made their way to Ingram Mall.

"What's up? When you gon' make this official?" Lexi asked

"Right now, I'm feeling you, half-breed."

She was so happy that she almost jumped in his lap trying to kiss him.

When they pulled up to the mall, the only thing that was on his mind was Lexi.

Ray Vinci

Chapter 6

Illy pulled up to Low-key's house to see what he could get into today. Illy knew that Low-key always had some hoes lined up, so that was the first place he went. As soon as he got out of his whip, two bad bitches drove by in a white Lexus and blew the horn.

"What's up, cutie?" the passenger yelled out of the window.

"Shit, you!" he yelled back.

He walked up to Illy's door and started pounding on the door like he was the police. Illy jumped back when Low-key swung the door open with an attitude.

"Damn, nigga, get the fuck up! It's1:00 p.m.!" said Illy.

"What the fuck, nigga? I should smoke yo' ass for bangin' on my shit like that."

"Yeah, whateva. What up though? Where the hoes at?" asked Illy.

Right before Low-key could answer, the same bad-ass bitches drove by again. When they got to the stop sign, Low-key ran to the street and tried to flag them down, but they kept going.

"Them hoes ain't tryna do nothing. I tried to get them hoes earlier," Illy said. "Go put some clothes on. I got some dank, so hurry up so we can smoke."

While Low-key went to put on some clothes, Illy sat on the porch and rolled up a couple of Sweets. He was wondering why Kilo hadn't call him back yet, so he picked up his phone and dialed his brother's number. It seemed like he answered on the first ring because Kilo was already talking.

"What's up, gangsta? Talk to me," Kilo said on the other end of the phone.

"Damn, nigga, you don't answer ya phone no more?" Illy asked. "What you got going on today?"

"Shit, I'm at the mall with Lexi. I might chill with her today."

"Alright, you ain't gon' be satisfied until Babygurl smoke both y'all," Illy said, laughing. "I'm at Low-key's spot. I'ma chill until I find something to get into."

"Bet. I'ma get at you, gangsta," Kilo said.

"Bet. Stay up. One love," he said, hanging up.

Illy looked up and saw the white Lexus pulling up in front of the house and he stood up. He walked towards the bar and couldn't help but think how li'l mama on the passenger side looked a lot like Alicia Keys. When she got out and stood on the side of the car, he really saw how bad she was.

She was 5'7" and weighed 145 pounds, but most of that came from all that ass and the big-ass titties she had, because her stomach had no fat. She was dressed in stone tight blue Levi's, a red and white Baby Phat shirt, and some black, red, and white Retro 5's

"Damn, li'l mama, you looking good as fuck. What's ya name?" Illy said

"Sasha," she said in a seductive tone.

"My name is Illy, and it's a pleasure to meet you," he said, eyeing her from head to toe. "What y'all got going on? 'Cause y'all keep riding by playing with a nigga."

"We tryna chill with you and ya homie. We ain't got nothing to do. We got a couple bottles of Ciroc if y'all got the weed," she said, being straight and looking at the blunts behind his ear.

"Let me go get my homeboy for ya homegirl so she can quit looking for him," he said, then took off jogging towards the house.

"Bitch, you think these niggas got something? 'Cause I ain't tryna waste my time," Sasha's friend said.

"If they don't, fuck it, bitch. Them niggas fine as hell, and at least we can get our pussies ate."

They both started laughing, then gave each other high fives. They had already started walking towards the house when Illy and Low-key came out. Low-key had on some navy-blue Dickie shorts, a white muscle T-shirt to show off his arms, and a navy blue and white Chargers snapback.

"And what might yo' name be, li'l mama?" Low-key asked.

"I'm Mandi," she said and then gave him a hug. Mandi was light-skinned with a nice sexy petite frame. Low-key was feeling her because she was rocking the shit out of them shorts, not to mention her green eyes and juicy lips.

"Let's take this inside," Low-key said. He went inside and the rest followed.

"Y'all chill and make y'all selves comfortable. The cups is in the kitchen. Blaze up this Sweet while I holla at my nigga real quick," said Illy.

"Don't take too long, 'cause I'm tryna get fucked up," Sasha said while licking her lips.

When Illy meet Low-key in the bedroom, Low-key instantly told him what was in his mind. "Stay on point, because these hoes seem too eager to kick it with us," said Low-key.

"I got you, but right now I'm tryna fuck something," Illy said, walking back to the living room.

By the time they made it back to the front, the girls were just pouring up everybody's cups. Mandi handed Low-key his and Sasha handed Illy his. Low-key lit up another blunt then put on some music and Sasha immediately started making her ass pop all over Illy. Illy went crazy when he saw how she was grinding on his dick.

Mandi was sitting on Low-key's lap facing him while grinding back and forth on his dick. Low-key and Illy were so caught up that they didn't even realize that they were the only ones drinking.

Before he knew it, Mandi was pulling down Low-keys pants. When his dick sprang out of his boxers, she jumped back because it was the biggest dick she had ever seen. She started jacking him off and wondering if she could get the whole thing in her mouth. She put those lips to use and started sucking the shit out of his dick while looking up at him. She used so much spit it felt like water running down his nuts.

Illy was about to start eating Sasha's pussy when he felt dizzy all of a sudden. When he looked up Sasha was smiling, because she knew that the handlebars she slipped in their drinks was kicking in. Before they knew it, they were both knocked out. Sasha jumped up quickly and started searching through Illy's pockets. She was surprised when she pulled out a stack of 20's and 50's, and when she counted it, it was $700.

"Jackpot!" Mandi reached in Low-key's pocket and found $500, a bag of doe-doe, and some handlebars. They were satisfied with what they had and left the house just like it was.

***

Low-key and Illy woke to being kicked by Babygurl.

"Wake up! I been tryna hit you up so fast, and you and this nigga knocked out with music blastin'!" Babygurl said to Low-key.

40

"Man, what the fuck?" Illy said, rubbing his head, trying to remember what happened.

"Them bitches robbed us, that's what happened," Low-key said, pissed off.

"Ha! Y'all mean to tell me y'all got robbed by bitches? That's what y'all get! Wait til Kilo hears this!"

"Say, I'ma chill for a li'l bit. My head spinning like a muthafucka," Illy told Low-key.

***

When Illy woke up, it was dark outside. He looked at his phone to see what time it was and it showed 1:30 a.m. All he could remember was that he'd gotten robbed by two bitches.

"Next time I see that bitch, she dead," he said out loud to himself. He was thirsty so he got to get something to drink. He forgot that he wasn't at his own crib when he saw Babygurl in the refrigerator, wearing just a thong and muscle T-shirt.

"Damn, girl, I didn't know you had all that." It slipped out of his mouth before he could catch it.

She jumped at the sight of him because she didn't realize he had stayed. "Boy, you scared the shit out of me!" she said, leaning against the counter. "You alright. Y'all was fucked up about being robbed." She noticed him looking between her legs. She started to close them but wanted to tease him. "You like what you see?" she asked him, then spread her legs wider.

"You betta chill out before Kilo kills both of us."

"Well, stop looking then!" she shot back. "Yo' li'l man must like what he sees."

"Don't start nothing you can't finish," he warned her.

For some reason, she was horny and said fuck it. "Let me see what you workin with?" she asked.

41

Illy wasted no time and pulled it out. She could tell that he was Kilo's little brother. In one motion, she dropped down and played with the head with her tongue. When she deep-throated him, he almost ran. She spit on his dick head, long-stroked him, and went into overtime. His eyes rolled in the back of his head and all he could hear was slurping noises. The whole time she had his dick in the back of her throat without breathing.

He stepped back and put her on the counter, then started sucking her titties. He finally made it to her pussy and licked and hummed on it at the same time. Once he started to tongue fucking her, she released on his tongue.

"Fuck me, please, I need that dick now!" she said while getting off the counter and turning around.

He rubbed his dick up and down her pussy, teasing her. She looked back to see what was going inside her and saw that it had gotten bigger. Illy rammed into her pussy with force, and every time he went in, he dug deeper and deeper.

"Oh yes! Fuck this pussy. Yes!"

Illy was loving the way Babygurl's ass was shaking. Her ass was super fat too be so small. He was pulling her hair and smacking her ass at the same time.

"You like this dick, don't you? I want you to bounce on this dick." He picked her up and put his dick right back in her.

She wrapped her legs around his back and did what he told her to do. When she started bouncing, she almost came off, but he had her locked.

"Oh shit! I'm cumming! I'm cumming! I'm cumming!" she screamed. It seemed like he was going deeper. She felt him in her stomach.

"Damn, this pussy good. I'm finna come."

She creamed on his dick one more time.

"I want to suck the cum out of this dick," she said while stuffing her mouth.

All it took was a few good pumps and he busted on her titties and face. When it hit him, he felt bad because Kilo was his bro and he had just fucked the girl he'd been with since he was thirteen.

"Don't tell Kilo about this," they both said at the same time, and then they both went their separate ways.

Ray Vinci

Chapter 7

Kilo, Slugga, and Felony sat in Chacho's, waiting on the rest of the Stick-Up Squad. It'd been two weeks since they pulled the lick off on Rico, but now they had a bigger one on their hands that needed to be done fast.

"Oh yeah, did you hear about them dumb-ass niggas Low-key and Illy?" Slugga asked Kilo.

"Naw, what happen to 'em?" Kilo asked. He knew it was something stupid if it had something to do with them two.

"Stupid asses got jacked by two bad-ass bitches!" Slugga said, laughing.

"What? You for real?" Kilo was all over the table laughing. Felony was rolling so hard that he had soda coming out of his nose.

Right when they calmed down from laughing, Illy, Low-Key, and Babygurl walked in and they started laughing again.

"What the fuck so funny?" Low-key asked.

"How the fuck y'all let two hoes jack y'all?" Felony asked, trying to hold back from laughing harder.

"Fuck y'all! When I see them hoes, I'ma smoke both of 'em. I put that on my momma!" Illy said, making his point clear.

"Alright, let's get down to business. I've been scoping out this lick on the Northside, but the thing is, it's a safe and it's a batch, so I'm gon' be the one who plays point guard."

"Why you gotta do it and not one of these broke dick-ass niggas?" Babygurl asked with jealousy in her voice.

"Because she only knows me, and them two niggas getting jacked instead of jacking," he told Babygurl with aggravation. "Anyways, this bitch is well connected to the Mexican Mafia, so we gotta be on point. They know nothing about us, and to-morrow she wants me to come over and chill with her. All I need y'all to do is to be one block away so y'all can help me with the safe."

"Do you know how much money it is in n the safe?" asked Slugga.

"Naw, I just know it's a lot of it," Kilo said. "Meet me on Skinnie's tomorrow at 7:00 p.m. and we gon' head out."

When Kilo was done explaining, Slugga's phone started ringing. While Slugga was on the phone, the squad was chopping it up about everything. Kilo noticed Babygurl looking at him, but he ignored her. He knew he was pissing her off, but he didn't care because he no longer had feelings for her.

"Say, Kilo, that was Crazy C. He said he can't afford the bricks right now but give him a week or two and he'll cop all five of 'em," Slugga said.

"Alright, I'm about to burn off. I'ma catch up with y'all tomorrow," said Kilo.

"Say, Babygurl, take my whip. I'ma roll with Slugga and Kilo. Don't have no niggas in my shit, and don't wreck my shit or I'ma smoke yo' ass," Illy said to Babygurl, then tossed her the keys. When they were walking out, she gave Illy a hug, then they left.

Kilo popped in an instrumental and he and Illy started rapping to the beat. Kilo and Illy had always known how to rap but were too caught up in the streets to do something with it. Slugga sat in the backseat and bobbed his head to what they were spitting.

"Say, what's up with you and Babygurl? Y'all getting friendly?" Kilo asked while his phone was ringing.

Illy never got the chance to answer because Kilo was already on the phone. "What's up, half-breed? Talk to me."

46

"My sister Lisa left her nigga and came to my house, and he's been over here beating on my door telling her to come out. He's got his homeboys with him, and he said if she don't come out when he get back, he gon' shoot up my shit!" Lexi said with a shaky voice.

"Just chill. I'm fifteen minutes away. I'll be right there," Kilo said. He hung up and pressed on the gas pedal.

"Y'all got y'all's bangas on y'all? These niggas tripping on Lexi's li'l sister, talking about shooting up her crib." said Kilo.

"Yeah," they both said while checking their clips.

It took them ten minutes to get to Lexi's spot, and when he pulled up, he saw four niggas in front of her shit, plus the whole neighborhood watching. Kilo jumped out followed by Illy and Slugga, then sat on the hood of the truck. Kilo got on his phone and told Lexi and her sister to come out and get in the truck. It took her no time to come out with her sister right behind her.

Before they could make it to the truck, one of the niggas grabbed Lisa by the arm and started yelling at her. Without thinking, Kilo and Slugga took off towards her.

"Say, homie, let li'l momma go before shit get out of hand," Slugga said to homeboy that had Lisa.

"Mind your business, bitch-ass nigga, before I beat yo' pussy ass out here!" he told Slugga.

Slugga laughed to himself, pulled his banga out, slid the clip out, and popped out the bullet that was in the chamber. As soon as he gave Kilo his clip, homeboy let Lisa go and charge at him. Slugga side-stepped him and slapped the shit out of him with the handle of his 9mm. Homeboy fell to the ground and Slugga was right on top of him with his pistol.

One of his homies tried to help him, and Kilo hit him with two of the hardest punches he'd ever thrown and knocked him out. Illy saw the other two pull out their straps, so he took his out and shot twice in the air. Slugga was still slapping ole boy with his gun and talking shit.

"Bitch! Ass! Nigga! Watch! Yo'! Fuckin'! Mouth! When! You! Talkin'! To! A! Gangsta!"

"Okay, that's enough!" Lisa yelled. "Let's go."

Before they got into the truck, Lisa kicked and spit on homeboy. Lexi got in the front while Kilo and Lisa got in the back with Slugga and Illy. As they rode back, Illy was laughing at what just went down.

"Say, gangsta, did you have to do homeboy like that?" Illy asked Slugga while laughing.

"Are you Okay? Thanks for helping me back there. My name is Lisa."

"Yeah, I'm good, and my name is Slugga."

"Y'all can stay at my crib tonight. 'Cause I know the laws gon' be at yo shit," said Kilo.

"Drop me off at Low-key's so I can get my whip from Babygurl," Illy said.

***

Kilo, Slugga, Lexi, and Lisa walked in the crib and went straight to the living room. Kilo pulled out a pack of doe-doe and rolled up, then told Lexi to go in the kitchen and pour some peach Ciroc. When Lexi came back, she sat next to Kilo and started kissing and hugging on him while Slugga and Lisa were getting to know each other.

"So, what's up? You gon' let me take ole boy's place? 'Cause obviously he don't know how to treat a pretty lady like she supposed to be treated," Slugga said, then sipped his drank.

"Damn, you got a mouthpiece. You got a bitch ready to fuck with you." She was feeling the weed. "Let me think, 'cause you got my head fucked up."

Kilo told them he was gone for the night and told Lexi to come to the bedroom when she was ready. She kicked it for a while, then made her way to the bedroom to go to sleep.

Ray Vinci

Chapter 8

Kilo woke up to his phone buzzing, and when he saw it was his li'l bro and what time it was, he let it go. He almost forgot Lexi was next to him until she raised up.

"What time is it, daddy?" Lexi asked.

"5:00 a.m." He kissed her on her forehead.

Lexi realized his dick was hard when he rolled over to hug her. Kilo hadn't had sex with her yet and she was starting to feel some type of way.

"Why you holding out on the dick?" she said while grabbing his shit.

"You ain't ready for all this. One shot and you'll be cooking me breakfast in the morning."

Lexi took that as a challenge. She got naked and was on top of him in an instant. Kilo was mesmerized by how beautiful she was, especially how fat her ass was. Kilo pulled down his boxers and Lexi jumped because she finally realized how big his dick was.

"Oh, my fuckin' God! What is that?" she asked, surprised. Kilo didn't even respond because he had a mouth fill of titties. "Please don't hurt me with this thing. It's been a long time."

She eased herself down on his dick little by little. When she realized she was only halfway on it and couldn't go down anymore, she just bounced on it.

"Oh, daddy, fuck! Sss," she moaned in his ear.

Kilo was so turned on by Lexi that he grabbed her ass and started making her bounce all the way on his dick.

"Kilo, daddy. Kilo, daddy, fuck your pussy. Make me cum on this dick!" Lexi was in ecstasy.

Kilo flipped her on her back and looked at her for a few seconds. He put his dick back in her and felt like he was stretching her even wider. She opened her legs, trying to take all of him, and he slammed into her, giving her every inch, he had. He dug so deep in her that he made her holler to the man up above. Soon the pain turned into pleasure and she came on his dick for the second time.

"Damn, baby, this pussy good and tight," Kilo moaned. "This daddy pussy, right?"

"Yes, daddy!"

Kilo put Lexi on all fours with her face in the pillows and her ass in the air, daring him to fuck the shit out of her. He slid in with slow strokes, enjoying the feel of her, then he moved faster and faster. Lexi was soaking wet, so it made it easier for him to move in and out, and she met him thrust for thrust.

"I'm cumming again, daddy, cum with me. Oh! I'm cumming!"

Kilo busted a nut at the same time, then Lexi lay on his stomach and gave him soft kisses on his face.

"I love you, daddy, I really do," she said.

"I love you too, half-breed."

They made love all morning until they fell asleep on top of each other.

***

Kilo woke up later that morning to the smell of breakfast and the sound of pots and pans. He got out of the bed, put on some basketball shorts, and made his way to the kitchen. When he got to the kitchen, Lexi was in his boxers and shirt talking to Lisa.

"Good morning, half-breed," he said, kidding her.

"Good morning, daddy," she said with a smile on her face.

"Damn, that nigga fine as hell," Lisa said to Lexi.

"Watch out, bitch, yours is in there." She pointed towards the living room.

"Damn, I get to wake up to breakfast in the morning? I told you the dick was good," he said while hugging her.

"Shit, I should be cooking you a whole damn buffet the way you had a bitch screaming," said Lexi. "You need to get that checked out, 'cause that is too gotdamn big."

Kilo started laughing and walked to the living room. He walked in and Lisa was caked up on Slugga.

"Y'all nasty! Get a room or something." he said flopping down on the couch.

"No you ain't talking about nobody being nasty the way you and Lexi was going at it last night. 'Oh daddy, I love you!'" he said, mocking Lexi.

"Fuck you," was all he could say, laughing at his homeboy.

While Kilo sat on the couch, he decided to hit Illy up. When Illy's phone went straight to voicemail, he tried again and it did the same thing. Kilo set his phone to the side as he heard a knock on the door.

As he went to answer it, Lexi was already letting Babygurl in. Babygurl had a stank look on her face when she walked in. She was fucked up about Lexi being in Kilo's shit when it should have been her.

"What the fuck is this shit y'all got going on up in here?" Babygurl asked Kilo while looking Lexi up and down.

"Don't start no shit, Babygurl. This my house. I do what the fuck I wanna do!" Kilo said. "What you doing over here so early anyways?" he asked, walking back to the living room. Before he could make it back to the living room, she was on the back of his heels. Kilo knew Babygurl didn't like what she was seeing, but he didn't care.

"Yo' brother is in jail for a gun charge. The police picked him up last night after he came to pick his car up. He been tryna call you all night, but I guess you been too busy," she said with her hands on her hips.

When Kilo sat down, she got annoyed because she knew he was fed up with her.

Before she could say something, Lexi walked in with his food. "Here you go, daddy. I got your drink coming to you in a little bit." She kissed him on his cheek, looking at Babygurl at the same time. She knew just how to piss Babygurl off, and she intended on doing just that.

"Thank you, half-breed."

"Y'all can make y'all own shit," she said to her sister and Slugga. "Do you want something to eat? I made plenty?" Lexi asked Babygurl.

"No, I don't!" Babygurl said with an attitude and rolled her eyes.

Lexi walked back to the kitchen right behind her sister, satisfied at how she made Babygurl feel.

"You got that bitch all up in yo' shit cooking breakfast, and she got your shit on. So what, y'all playing house and shit now?" she yelled, making sure Lexi heard every word. Babygurl was mad and she was about to let Kilo know how just how mad she was. He had her fucked up if he thought she was just gon' let some random bitch come and take her place.

"Why the fuck you worried about it? What we had is done. You fucked that up, remember? And this my shit. I can playhouse and do whateva the fuck I wanna do!" said Kilo.

She didn't have a chance to say something before Lexi was on his side.

"Look, bitch, mind your damn business, 'cause this right here is mines," Lexi said, ready to do whatever. You could tell she was mad.

Before she knew it, Babygurl was lunging towards her, but Kilo was quick and grabbed her. When he carried her to the kitchen, Slugga and Lisa were wondering what had happened.

"What the fuck is wrong with you? You better chill the fuck out before you piss me off. Go wait in the car while I get dressed so we can go get my brother out," Kilo said with anger in his voice then walked back to the living room while she walked out the door. When Kilo got back to Lexi, she was crying and explaining to Lisa what happened.

"Lexi, let me holla at you in my room," he said, then walked off.

When she walked in, he was getting dressed.

"You mad at me, daddy?" she asked.

"Naw, why would I be mad at you? You didn't do nothing wrong," he said while hugging her.

"Where you going? I wanna go."

"I'm going to get my stupid-ass brother out of jail, and no you can't go because she taking me."

"Why she gotta take you? Fuck that bitch." she said.

"Because she giving up half on the bail and we using her name," said Kilo. "Here goes my keys and some money. Go do something with yo' sister before she fall in love with Slugga," he said, smiling.

They kissed, then made their way back up front.

***

"What's up, Illy, what you got on yo' mind?" asked Illy's celly, looking at the eighteen-year-old curiously.

"Shit, my big bro should be coming to get me out in a bit," he said. He was trying to get out before they hit the lick, because he was broke with no car so he felt like he had to start over. He was so lost in his thoughts that he didn't hear the Bossman call his name over the intercom.

"Illy, bitch, they calling yo name for RCO1," his celly said snapping him out of his thoughts.

Illy jumped up quick, grabbed all his shit, and then bolted out of the door. Everybody was yelling at him, but he paid no attention to them. When he got to booking, it was packed and it smelled like feet and ass, but fuck it, he was leaving this bitch anyways.

It felt like it took them forever to release him from jail. As soon as he stepped out, he saw Kilo and Babygurl.

"What's up, big bro?" he said while giving him some dap.

"What's good, gangsta? Damn, you stink. Did you shower or what?" Kilo said, covering up his nose.

"Fuck you. What's up, Babygurl? Thank you for bailing me out."

Babygurl didn't say anything and walked back to the car.

"What's wrong with her?"

"Long story. Let's go so we can be ready tonight."

Chapter 9

Correy was sitting in his truck outside of Ray-Ban store off of Eisenhower when he saw the baddest redbone he had ever seen in his life. Li'l mama had a face like Eve and a body like Trina's. She stood at 5'6" and 120 pounds with long hair, not to mention she was dressed to kill. When she walked by, Correy was damn near falling out his window trying to holla at her.

"Damn! What's up, li'l mama? Slow down and stop acting like you don't see a nigga damn near about fall out this window," he said. "What's yo' name?"

"My name is Keisha, and what you doing sitting out here anyways?" she asked while laughing at him.

"Shit, counting this money and rolling up this loud," he said, not boasting.

When he said that, she started flirting extra hard. "Damn, balla, can a bitch chill with you?"

"Jump in and smoke something with me."

She walked to the other side, then got in. Correy passed her the Sweet and started chopping it up with her. Before he knew it, she was giving him some head. He never noticed the two niggas creeping up on the side of his truck. When he felt the cold steel behind his ear, he jumped, causing Keisha to choke on his dick.

"Come off everything you got, bitch-ass nigga!" homie with the gun to his head said.

Correy said nothing. He just went in his pockets and gave everything he had.

"This all you got, nigga? You riding around this bitch like you got bank, broke-ass nigga!" He was mad because all he got was $500, two zones of crack, and some weed.

Correy was so caught up on homeboy that he didn't notice Keisha get out. By the time he realized it, all three of them were gone. All he could do was sit back and laugh at what just happened. He lit up a Newport, started up his truck, and went to cop some more work. He was glad he didn't bring all his money with him because he just about to score a brick.

He thought about all the mistakes they had made, but the only one that mattered was that bitch, because he knew he would see her again. He picked his phone to call Philly, but was stopped by Philly calling him.

"What up, Joe, what's good with you?" Correy asked.

"I thought you was coming through. Where you at?" asked Philly.

"I'm about to get some more bread right now and I'm on my way." He started telling Philly what just went down, but he didn't want to hear no long-ass speech.

"Alright, hurry up," Philly said and then hung up.

Correy called Lovey to let her know he was on his way and to bring the cash out. As soon as he pulled up, Lovey brought the cash out, then he kissed her and peeled out. Before he turned out of the gates, he saw something out of the corner of his eye. He knew he wasn't tripping when he saw that same bitch Keisha and one of the niggas that had just robbed him. He smiled to himself because not even forty-five minutes ago, they set him up and now he knew where they lived. He wanted to go blast on them right then and there, but he had shit to do. He made a mental note for later that night.

***

When Correy got to Philly's house, he saw Tidy's silver drop top Mercedes. When he got out to walk to the door, Tidy was already opening it up.

"What up, nigga?" he asked Correy while shaking his hand.

"Shit, tryna get to this money," he said. "I gotta keep up with you niggas some kind of way."

When he got in the house, all he could smell was doe-doe. As soon as he got in, he reached for the Sweet Tidy had.

"Where that nigga Philly at?"

When he said that, Philly was coming out of the back.

"About time you made it. We was about to leave and go to the mall to get something to wear for tonight's show," Philly said.

"I would go with y'all, but I didn't bring no money and I got people waiting on me."

"What you need so we can go?" he asked while hitting the blunt.

"Damn, Joe. You always in a rush. Slow down some time," Correy said while pulling out a knot of money. "Let me get a block for right now."

After they made the exchange, Correy, Tidy, and Philly chopped it up for a while. While they were in the middle of saying their goodbyes, Correy's phone rang.

"What's up? Talk to me, what you need?"

"Say, baby boy, this Quick. You told to hit you up when I got out."

Quick had been Correy's celly when he went to jail. He had actually got real tight with him. They used to stay up and ride all night, so he knew him real well.

"What up. Joe? I was just thinking about you. I need you out here nigga!" he said with excitement.

"Come scoop me up. I'm over here on Austin Highway in the Landings," Quick said.

"Bet. Don't go nowhere. I'm coming," he said, then hung up the phone. "Say, I gotta go. I'ma holla at y'all later on."

On the way to Austin Highway, he was thinking about how badly he needed a right-hand man, and Quick was just the right person for the job. Quick was a gangsta and a hustla, so he was a great prospect to him.

He pulled into the Landings and spotted Quick ASAP. Quick was dark chocolate, 6'0", weighed 185 pounds, and had braids that went down to his shoulders. Correy couldn't do anything but shake his head, because the girl he was talking to walked off rolling her eyes. He knew the only reason she did that was because he was looking bummed out, because he knew how to pull hoes. He blew the horn to get his attention. Quick jumped up, giving him dap.

"What's up, baby boy? Damn, you doing ya thing out of here. I'm doing bad. I need you," Quick said while checking him out.

"Don't worry, I got you, just stick around. But first let's get you out of this shit." He was eyeing his clothes.

***

Kilo was waiting on Felony to get there with the shit that that they needed for the safe. As soon as he was about to ask where he was, he walked through the door.

"You got everything?" he asked Felony.

"Yeah, I got a dolly and a torch."

60

"Alright, y'all gon' wait for me three houses down while I get everything ready. Illy, I'ma hit yo phone to let y'all know when I'm ready. Kilo explained, then left to head to the other side of town. Forty-five minutes later, Kilo pulled up with Veronica in front of her house. When he pulled up, he looked in his rearview mirror and spotted his squad three houses down. He got out of his truck and was greeted by a beautiful Mexican woman. She was in a nightgown, but you could tell she had a banging body, plus her long blonde hair made her look like a white girl. He gave her a hug and a kiss and at the same time he could feel Babygurl's eyes on him on the side of his head.

"I hope I'm here to have a good time, 'cause it sho' seems like it," he said while looking her up and down.

"Oh, you will. Let's go in and chill," she said while walking inside.

Kilo walked right behind her and he really saw how much she had because her shit was fly. "Damn, girl, you paid like a muthafucka," said Kilo.

"I told you my brothers fuck with the Mexican Mafia."

All Kilo could think about was how much the dumb-ass bitch ran her mouth.

"Why don't you make yourself comfortable? My brothers won't be home for a while. We can do whatever you want."

He looked at his watch and it was 8:30 p.m. so he had to get this show on the road. "What you got to drink?" he asked.

"I got Ciroc, Grey Goose, Gin, E&J. Whatever."

"I'll take some Ciroc."

"I got you, baby," she said, then poured his drink. "You know, I never been with a black guy before.

"Well, you in for a ride," he said as he sat down and took off his shirt.

61

When she came in, she had the two glasses in her hand. She paused and looked at Kilo and couldn't help but to stare. "Damn, you fine."

"Come sit down next to daddy."

She downed her drink and sat next to Kilo. He started sipping his drink, but he didn't want to get too fucked up. She was rubbing Kilo's body, tipsy off of the Ciroc.

"Let me see your dick." She licked her lips.

He said nothing as he unzipped his pants and pulled down his boxers. His dick sprang out, standing straight at attention.

"Oh my God, that thing is huge," she said with her eyes popped out of her head. She grabbed it with both hands, then started jacking him off. "Can I suck it?" she asked.

"Only if you do a good job."

She went to work but could only get half of it in her mouth before she started choking.

"Wait, let's take this to the room. I'ma fix us another drink while you get ready."

When he got back, she was butt naked on the bed waiting for him. He handed her the drink and she drank it in one gulp.

"Now come fuck me, papi."

He wasted no time and dove headfirst into the pussy. He could tell the pills he put in her drink were working because she fell asleep as soon as he was done.

***

"Damn, what's taking this nigga so long to call?" asked Illy.

"He probably knee deep in the pussy. That bitch was fine as hell," said Felony.

"She was fine," Low-key added.

"Y'all shut up before I smoke him and that bitch right now," Babygurl said with hostility in her voice.

It seemed like they were waiting for hours until Slugga saw a red F150 pull up in front of the same house Kilo was in.

"Say y'all, what's that?" asked Slugga

"Ain't that the same house Kilo went in?" asked Felony.

"Yeah!" Babygurl said.

Two big Mexicans jumped out of the truck followed by a white bitch. When they started walking up the driveway, they jumped out and ran down the sidewalk as quickly and quietly as possible. Right when one was about to open the door, Felony had the banga to his head.

"Don't move, gangsta, or I'll blow ya skulls to pieces."

"What the fuck is this? Do you know who you fucking with, niggas?"

"I don't give a fuck. What I want you to do is walk in slow."

Before they could open the door, the brother jumped and hit Felony behind the head, and Low-key slapped him with a pump shotgun.

"Get the fuck in the house!" Low-key yelled. When they opened the door, they heard screams and moaning coming from the back and seconds later, Kilo came from the back.

"I was just about to call y'all," he said, looking at the three strangers.

Slugga went to get the torch and dolly from my truck." He took off and came back as they tied the nigga up in the basement. They went to the room and saw ole girl naked on the bed knocked out. He handed Kilo the torch and he went to work, and it took him only ten minutes. They loaded it up and left the house like they were never there.

***

When Lovey woke up, she heard the TV on in the living room. She figured she'd left it on when she went to bed. She had stayed up all night waiting on Correy, but when she woke up, he was asleep next to her.

When she walked in the living room, she jumped at the sight of Quick. He was sitting on the couch in his boxers, and Lovey couldn't help but stare because the nigga was fine. When she realized he was staring back, she went back in the bedroom because she only had on her bra and panties.

"Correy, wake up. Who the fuck is in my living room?" she asked while shaking him out of his sleep.

"That's my nigga Quick. He gon' kick it for a while until he gets on his feet."

"Well, the nigga scared the shit out of me. You hungry?"

"Yeah."

When they walked in the living room, Quick had already put on his clothes.

"What up, Joe?"

"What up with it, gangsta? I appreciate the clothes."

"No problem. You was looking like a bum."

"Fuck you, nigga. I'm sorry if I scared li'l mama."

"I'm good," she said before Correy could say something.

"Lovey this Quick, Quick this Lovey."

"You hungry, Quick?" she asked.

"Yeah. Thank you. Smoke something."

Correy pulled out a blunt of doe-doe as if he knew what he was gon' say. He went in the kitchen and lit it on the stove, and let Lovey hit it a few times, then went back in the living room. While they smoked, he told Quick about the bitch and two niggas that ran down on him.

"When we get done here, we gon' handle that and from there, I'ma put you on."

Ray Vinci

Chapter 10

They sat in front of her apartment passing a blunt back and forth. They had been sitting in front for about forty-five minutes when Correy finally saw the door open. When he saw li'l mama walk out then walk back inside, he knew she was alone.

"Look, you gon' walk by her apartment and when she come out, she gon' holla at you 'cause you look like money. When you get in, leave the door unlocked and I'ma come in behind you, then I'll take it from there," Correy explained.

While Correy was explaining everything to Quick, Keisha stepped outside to smoke a cigarette.

"Damn, baby bad as hell!" he said while checking his banga.

Before Correy could say something, Quick was already out of the truck walking towards Keisha. He knew he had a soldier on his team, but he also knew he was weak for hoes. As Quick approached her, just like Correy said, she spoke.

"What's up, chocolate, how you doing?" she asked Quick while checking him out.

"I'm good. What's yo' name, li'l mama?"

"I'm Keisha. What might yours be?"

"Quick. You know where to get some weed from? I'll smoke a couple of Sweets with you."

"How about I smoke with *you*. Come in," she said, then walked inside.

He looked towards Correy and smiled because he knew he was doing the same thing.

When he stepped in, he couldn't help but think how stupid the bitch was. Her crib was alright. It had clothes everywhere and a mattress was in the living room like somebody had just gotten out of it.

"Let's go to my room," she said walking towards the back.

He followed her to the back while watching her ass giggle through the boxers she had on. He sat on the bed and while she went in the closet to get the weed, the whole time he was looking at her ass. When she came out with the weed, she saw that his dick was hard.

"Damn, boy, you must really like what you see," she said, then she sat next to him

"Hell yeah!" he said while pulling out his dick.

She knew what she had to do to get what she wanted, so she went to work on him. Correy walked through the house and went straight to the back. When he got to the bedroom, he had his banga in his hand.

"I see you don't hesitate on sucking dick to get what you want," he said.

Keisha looked up with Quick's dick still in her mouth. When she realized who he was, she started explaining ASAP.

"They made me do it, I swear!" she explained with her hands in the air.

"Get up. I ain't trippin' on you, but I do want you to call those bitch-ass niggas," he said

"Okay, just don't hurt me." She grabbed her phone and dialed a number and it took a while before she got an answer.

"Jay, I got this mean-ass lick for you," she said. He must've said Okay, because she was off the phone fast.

"You know, a nigga could use you," Correy said.

"I can use some money and a down-ass nigga," she said, looking at Quick.

They heard the door open and they both pulled out their straps.

"Baby, I'm in here!" she yelled, on point.

When he walked in, Correy slapped him with his pistol.

"Bitch, you set me up!"

"No, she didn't. She did what she had to do to survive," Correy said. "Come off everything."

Everything he had, Correy split with Quick and Keisha, then Quick pistol whipped him until he wasn't moving. He, Quick, and Keisha left with money on their minds.

Ray Vinci

Chapter 11

"Hello!" Lexi yelled through her phone because she didn't want to turn down the music.

"Girl, turn that shit down!" Kilo yelled from the other end of the phone.

She reached and turned the music down and at the same time pulled up in front of Lovey's house.

"Where you at with my truck?" He knew it wasn't good to let her use the truck, but they wanted to see their sister, so he let them.

"I just pulled up at my sister's house."

"Be careful, and don't crash my shit."

"Okay, I'ma call you later on when I'm on my way back," she said, then hung up the phone. She loved Kilo so much and she knew he loved her because he was always worried. They had moved in with each other, so their relationship was already on the next level. He had gave her some money to go out with her sisters, and that's exactly what she was gon' do.

When she and Lisa stepped out of the truck, they looked across the apartments and saw a whole bunch of polices. Before they could say something, Lovey opened the door and answered what they were thinking.

"Some nigga got beat to death," said Lovey. "Come on before it gets too late."

They jumped back in the truck and smashed off. Lexi wanted to see what was going on, so she drove by the apartment. When she drove by, she saw the ME's carrying out a body.

"Damn, somebody did that nigga bad. Whateva he did, I bet he regret that shit now!" said Lisa.

"I know, right?"

They all busted out laughing as Lexi turned out of the apartments.

"Where y'all tryna go right now?" Lexi asked.

"Shit, I'm hungry," Lisa said. "Let's go to Chacho's."

"Hell yeah, and then we can go to Cocoa's Lounge and get our drink on," said Lovey.

"Somebody roll some weed up," Lexi said. They had made it inside of Chacho's and went to sit in the back. They ordered a big plate of nachos and talked about every nigga that came through.

"Damn, bitch, slow down! You eating like you pregnant!" Lovey said to Lexi.

Lexi's eyes got big like she was surprised at what Lovey said. In fact, she did think she was pregnant but she didn't want anybody to know until she was sure and knew how Kilo felt about it. They had known each other for years but had only been sexing each other a little less than a month

"Why you say it like that?" she asked calmly.

"Because you eating all the damn food... Wait." Lovey stopped in the middle of her sentence. "BITCH, YOU PREG-NANT!"

"Damn, bitch, shut up! What, you want everybody to know?" said Lexi.

"I knew you was gon' get knocked up because Kilo be having that ass screaming all night," Lisa said while laughing.

"Okay, okay, I'm pregnant, but don't tell nobody until I let Kilo know," Lexi said, making sure they understood her.

They sat at the table and talked until it got dark outside. Once they got in the truck, she turned up the music and headed towards Cocoa's Lounge. On the way, she thought about what Kilo would think about her being pregnant. She also thought about what it would be like with a baby and she was happy.

Her thoughts was interrupted by Lovey and Lisa yelling at her.

"Bitch, you passed the club up!" they both screamed over the music. She did a U-turn and entered the parking lot. It was jam packed with niggas and hoes and they planned on having fun. Cocoa's Lounge was for grown-ups to come and chill and get their drink on without the drama.

"Since this my last time drinking, I'm gonna get wasted," Lexi said, getting out of the truck. She knew that she was being reckless, but she wanted one last drink if she was indeed pregnant.

"You got that right," said Lisa

They walked towards the door and it seemed like all the niggas were breaking their necks to see them. They knew they were bad and strutted just to make every bitch there was jealous. Once they got inside, they sat on the couches that were closer to the bar.

It seemed like it took no time for niggas to start laying their mack down. Niggas were sending them drinks from way across room. Even though they gave nobody no play, they still loved all the attention they were getting.

"Girl, this morning I woke up and saw this fine-ass chocolate nigga in my living room in his boxers," Lovey told her sisters.

"You need to stop. Correy gon' fuck yo' ass up," said Lisa.

"That nigga too busy to give me some dick. Might as well get it from somebody else," she said while giving a high five to Lexi.

"You got that right," said Lexi. "Girl, this Moscato is good."

They sat and talked about everything. They were close and only had each other. Their mother and father had passed away a couple of years ago, and their brother was in prison serving twenty-five years for murder.

"Bitch, it's 10:00 p.m. I gotta get Kilo's truck back."

"Damn, time flies by when you having fun," Lovey said.

They grabbed their purses, paid the tab, and headed to the door. Before they made it to the truck, Lexi noticed a familiar face heading her way. When the girl got closer, she knew who it was automatically. Babygurl walked up with another Mexican girl who was taller than her.

"What's up now, bitch? Kilo ain't here to save yo' ass now!" Babygurl told Lexi in Spanish.

"Bitch, I don't got time for yo' childish-ass games," she said. Lexi knew she was too tipsy to fight, and she didn't want to put her baby in jeopardy over a jealous-ass bitch.

"Hold up, who is this bitch, Lexi?" asked Lovey.

"I'm Babygurl, and you need to mind yo' fucking business."

"First of all, this is my business. Second, watch how you talking to me and my sisters before I set this bitch off," Lovey said with anger in her voice.

"Let's go, sis, before we go to jail, and besides, I can't fight this hoe with Kilo's baby in me right now." Lexi knew exactly what to say to piss Babygurl off.

As soon as she said it, Babygurl's face turned beet red. She was moving towards Lexi, but the bouncers was already grabbing her and carrying her out of the door.

74

"Everybody not gon' be able to save yo' ass. Just wait. I got something for you!" she yelled out at Lexi, meaning every word she said.

The bouncers made sure they were straight before he let them leave. As they were walking towards the truck, Lexi pulled out her phone and called Kilo. It didn't take long for him to answer because she started talking fast.

"I ran into yo' li'l bitch at the club."

"Gotdamn, Babygurl just don't like yo' ass, huh?" Kilo said jokingly.

"I'm serious! I started to whoop her ass, but I didn't want to fuck up my night."

"I'm just playing. Where are you at?" asked Kilo.

"I'm leaving the club——"

Before she could finish her sentence, shots riddled the back of the truck. Lexi swerved out of the parking lot and into the street. She sped down the street only to be followed by a black car. She thought it was Babygurl until the car sped up and along the side of them. When she saw that it was a car full of niggas, her heart started pumping faster and faster. When she looked and saw a gun pointing her way, she turned off on a side road. She guessed the niggas didn't shoot anymore because they saw who it was. She knew they were looking for Kilo and she was scared to death. When she was out of sight, she had finally calmed down.

"Are y'all okay?" she asked her sisters.

"Yeah, we straight. What the fuck just happened?" Lovey asked.

"I don't know, but we sho'll gon' find out when get to Kilo. After that bullshit, I need something to smoke," said Lexi.

Lisa was in the back already rolling up a Swisher Sweet. Lexi's phone was ringing the whole time everything was going down, but she decided not to answer it. She was gon' wait until she got home to find out what happened.

***

When Lexi and her sisters pulled up to the house, Kilo and his squad were already on the porch waiting. Even Babygurl was there. When she got out of the truck, Kilo walked to her in a fast pace.

"What the fuck happened? Who was shooting at you?" Kilo asked her.

"I don't know! Whoeva it was thought I was you because when they saw me, they sped off, so you tell me," said Lexi. "And what the fuck is she doing here?"

"I called my squad because you was getting shot at." Kilo was mad about what happened to Lexi and he intended on finding out who was out to get him.

He and Lexi along with her sisters walked to the porch where his squad was. As soon as they stepped on the porch, everybody could feel the tension Babygurl and Lexi had with each other. Kilo wanted to let them get it out of their systems but thought twice because he knew Babygurl would tear Lexi a new asshole. When Lisa saw Slugga, she ran up to him and hugged him. Lovey was caught by surprise to see her sister like that.

"And what do we have here?" Lovey asked.

"This my baby Slugga. Slugga, this is my sister Lovey."

"How you doing, Lovey? I'm glad y'all alright," Slugga said.

"Say, are you gon' take me home or what?"

"You can stay here for tonight and we can take you home on the morning," said Lexi.

With everything situated, everybody went their separate ways. Lexi was glad Babygurl didn't trip to make things worse and felt even better that she didn't say anything about her being pregnant.

Ray Vinci

Chapter 12

Kilo, Lexi, and Lovey along with Lisa and Slugga pulled up in front of Lovey's apartment. As they parked, Kilo turned down the music, and at the same time Correy walked out with Quick right behind him. It seemed like when Correy walked out, Kilo's eyes connected with his and they started staring each other down. He was also watching Quick because he'd never seen him before. He didn't know why he was nervous about being here, but he was. Lexi and Lisa saw the tension and started talking to Kilo, but he wasn't even listening. All Kilo could see was the two niggas standing in front of the door.

An instant thought popped into his head about how much money the nigga was getting, so he made a mental note to check the nigga out. Lexi and Lisa got out of the truck to say what's up to Correy and that's when Slugga broke his train of thought.

"What's up, gangsta, what you got on yo' mind? You ain't said shit the whole time we've been here." said Slugga.

"How much money you think that nigga getting?" asked Kilo.

"I don't know, but it's whateva with me."

"Just chill, gangsta. Let me find some shit about him first," Kilo said with a smile on his face. Kilo rolled down the window, then started talking to Lexi.

"What's up, half-breed what you gon' do? I gotta meet up with my bro in a li'l bit."

"I'ma chill with Lovey for a little while," she said.

"Cool, call me when you ready."

They gave them some bread, then drove off. Before he drove off, he saw Correy nodding his head and smiling. He smirked backed, turned his music up, and then headed towards the east side.

***

"What's up, nigga? Where the fuck you at? We been waiting on yo' ass all morning?" Illy yelled through the phone.

"Shut up, nigga, I'm down the street. I had to get some squares and some cigars." Kilo replied.

"Well, hurry up, because I'm ready to smoke. I know you got some heat."

"Alright," he said, then hung up.

Slugga was sitting in the passenger seat laughing while rolling a Sweet. "That nigga Illy think he running shit," Slugga said while lighting the blunt.

"I know. He gon' make me whoop his ass." Kilo started thinking about how his li'l bro was all he had and remembered the day he promised to take care of him.

Slugga passed him the blunt as they pulled up to Low-key's house. When they pulled up, Felony was sitting on the porch talking on the phone. "Damn, let a nigga hit the weed?" Felony asked and then Kilo passed him the Sweet.

"What's up? Anybody talk on the streets about who tryna get at me?" Kilo asked Felony.

"Naw, but some niggas just shot up Low-key's spot this morning," he said while hitting the Sweet.

"Word?" was all Slugga could say. Kilo started to say something, but decided not to and just walked inside.

"What's up, gangsta, where Low-key at?" he asked Illy while showing him some love.

"He in the back rolling up some of that boo boo-ass weed he got. I just came from back there and the nigga on some shoot 'em up bang bang shit. He say he know who did it."

"I'm finna go holla at that nigga right now. Slugga and Felony out there blowing if you wanna hit the weed," he said, then headed to Low-key's room.

When Kilo walked in the room, Low-key and Babygurl were chopping it up with each other. He was rolling blunts while she was breaking down the cigars. His eyes locked with hers and you could tell they still had feelings for each other.

"Nigga, did you hear what I said?" Low-key yelled at Kilo.

"Naw, what up, nigga?"

"We gon' ride on them bitch-ass niggas from the club."

"Who was them niggas anyways?" he asked.

"Some niggas called Block Boys, tryna make a name for they self, but on my momma, we gon' smoke them pussies."

Babygurl lit up a blunt hit it a few times then passed it to Low-key. They let each other know what was gonna go down, then Kilo left back to the porch. When Kilo got outside, Illy was bumping Li'l Wayne. He stopped and told Felony to find out what he could about Correy, then get back to him. As soon as he and Slugga got back in the truck, his phone started ringing. He looked at the number and didn't recognize it, so he let it ring. As soon as he turned the music up, Slugga's phone started ringing.

"What's up, sexy?" Slugga said through the phone.

"Nothing; just thinking about you," a female voice said.

"Where you at? Me and my nigga tryna come chill."

"I'm in Stone Oak with my cousin," she said.

"We on our way," he said, then hung up. "Say, let's go fuck with my li'l hoe and her cousin."

Kilo jumped on I-35 and headed to Stone Oak.

***

Kilo pulled into the liquor store on the corner and got out. When he came back, he had two bottles of peach Ciroc in his hand.

"Might as well get fucked up. We ain't got shit else to do," said Kilo.

"Alrighty."

When they pulled up to the apartment, he turned his music down, then turned his truck off.

"Hold up, let me call her and let her know we here." He got on the phone. "Say, li'l mama, I'm outside."

"Okay," she said, then hung up.

The door opened and she waved them inside. When they got inside it was cool and the apartment was laid back.

"Hey, I'm Valarie," she said while shaking his hand.

"I'm Kilo. I brought something for y'all to sip on, if it's cool."

She grabbed the bottles and went to the kitchen. Kilo couldn't help but stare because all she had on was a long t-shirt, and she was sexy as hell.

"Damn, where you find baby at? She look like she bad under that shirt," said Kilo.

"She is bad, but she's off limits. Wait till you see her cousin. She pretty as hell, plus that ass is fat."

Kilo went to the couch. He sat down and felt at ease about being there. He was lost in his thoughts but was brought back when the door opened. He put his hands under shirt because his survival instinct kicked in.

"Valarie!" someone yelled while coming in.

When he saw who it was he relaxed. He couldn't help but stare because she looked like Mariah Carey with a body like Buffie. She was 5'3" with blonde hair with brown streaks in it. When he saw that she had green eyes, his mouth almost dropped. Valarie came out of the kitchen and took her in the bedroom.

"Oh my God, who is that fine dude standing in your living room?" Bianca asked.

"That's Slugga's homeboy. They came to chill."

"Well, I'm finna go see what's up," she said, then took off.

They chilled and got to know each other. You could tell Bianca was feeling him because she was all over him. They kicked it until they had to leave, but they exchanged numbers, hoping to see each other again.

Ray Vinci

Chapter 13

Quick woke up and looked at his phone and it was 2:48 a.m. His head was pounding and all he could remembered was he and Correy dropping off Lovey's sisters. The only reason he was up because he had to take a piss. He hurried up and ran to the restroom. He was just getting through when Lovey opened the door. When she saw Quick with his dick in his hand, she just stood there staring. She thought to herself that he had to be every bit of twelve inches.

"Not bad," she said, then closed the door.

He finished doing what he had to do then went back to his room. He didn't know what to think of the situation that just happened. Lovey was fine as hell and he wanted to fuck, but Correy was his homeboy. He decided he wasn't gon' fuck and he wasn't gon' tell Correy neither. Before he knew it, he was falling back to sleep.

***

Correy and Quick were sitting in the trap. They had just got off of Austin Highway and Deerwood. Today was slow as hell. His phone wasn't ringing, and the trap was new so dope-fiends were hardly coming by.

"Say, my nigga, I'm finna walk around the apartments to see if it's some money around here," Quick said, walking towards the door.

"Hold up, Joe, I'ma roll with you. Let me grab my banga."

When they stepped on the porch, it was jumping. There were so many niggas and hoes that it made Correy nervous.

They hit a few corners to meet a few dopefiends and gave them the address and phone numbers. When they were headed back, Quick noticed a tall dark-skinned nigga staring at them. He clutched his 9mm and was about to tell Correy until his phone rang.

"What up, talk to me."

"Where you at? I got a client that wants three zones. I started to rob the nigga, but decided to bring him to y'all," Keisha said.

"We on Deerwood. Bring him through and call me when you get here," he said and then hung up. When he got off the phone, they were already at the apartment.

"Keisha on her way with a nigga that wants three zones." he told Correy. "Did you see that nigga staring at us?"

"Naw, did it look like he wanted to do something?"

"Naw, but I can tell he was a stand-up nigga, and I don't trust him."

"Just chill. He might not trust us neither, but we gon' keep a close eye on him."

Correy had his mind on how he was gon' turn this bitch into a gold mine, but he needed more niggas on his team to make it happen.

***

"Bitch, I'm telling you, the nigga had a third leg down there," said Lovey.

"Alright, you ain't gon' be satisfied," said Lexi. Lexi and Lovey were chilling at hers and Kilo's house smoking.

"So, when you gon' tell Kilo he got a baby on the way?"

"Tonight, after I put this pussy on him."

They fell deep in conversation but were cut short when they heard a car pull up. They didn't know who it was until Felony got out.

"What's up, y'all, where Kilo?" he asked.

"He didn't come home last night. Wanna hit the weed?" Lexi asked.

"Yeah," he said, sitting down.

The whole time they were talking, they never noticed the black Monte Carlo circling the block. Lovey stood up to go in the house. The car stopped then the back window rolled down. Felony saw the muzzle of a shotgun and pushed Lovey in the house and dove on Lexi as they rolled off the porch. As soon as he did that, shots were let off and he was hit in the left calf muscle. Felony screamed as he felt the buck shots. He told Lexi to go around the back and call Kilo, then pulled out his 40 cal. When the shots stopped, he let the shooter have it. He hit him once in the neck and again in the head. He was dead on impact. He never saw the nigga come from the other side. He got hit in the shoulder and twice in the stomach. Felony dropped instantly and they sped off.

"Hold on, the ambulance is on the way," Lexi told Felony when she ran to him.

Lexi and Lovey stayed by his side until they showed up.

Ray Vinci

Chapter 14

When Kilo woke up, it was 4:00 p.m. He looked around and noticed where he was, then reached for his phone. He and Slugga came back after they realized it was too late to drive. Bianca walked in the room in her panties and bra with a plate and some Kool-Aid.

"I thought you might be hungry, so I made you a sandwich and some Kool-Aid," Bianca said.

"I appreciate that," he said while grabbing the plate. "Where are my clothes?"

"Over there," she said, pointing to a chair in the corner "You passed out on me last night, so I laid you down. Oh, and your gun is in the closet if you want it.

"I'll get it before I leave. Is my phone in my pants?" he asked, knowing it was since it was nowhere around.

She didn't even answer him. She wanted him to finish his food. She loved the way he looked, from his skin to his smile. She grabbed the plate and cup, then took it back to the kitchen. When she came back, he was standing up searching his pockets.

"It's all there," she said.

"Naw, it's cool," he said while staring at her. She was beautiful and thick as hell. He didn't notice he was staring until he felt his dick getting hard.

She walked up on him and kissed him while stroking his dick through his boxers. She sat him down in the chair and kissed him on his neck all the way to his stomach. At the same time, she was pulling down his boxers.

"Damn you got a big thick-ass dick," she said while jacking him off. She wasted no time wrapping her lips around his shaft and started sucking the shit out of his dick.

She looked up at him and all he saw was green eyes and those beautiful lips wrapped around his manhood. Bianca was trying to stuff the whole thing in her mouth, but only got halfway. Kilo pulled her up and started for the bed, but she pushed him back down then straddled him. She grabbed his dick and guided herself on it. She bounced on it slow and easy because it felt like he was ripping her pussy into two.

Kilo's dick was white because she came all over it.

"Oh! Baby, I just came, fuck me!" she moaned in Kilo's ear.

Kilo grabbed her ass cheeks and made her come all the way down. He bounced her down so hard that she jumped off. He stood up, bent her over the chair, then slid his dick back in.

"Oh, fuck yeah! Fuck this pussy! Make me cum! Oh, I'm cumming again!" she yelled.

"You like daddy dick, don't you? Who pussy is this?" he said while smacking her ass and pulling her hair.

"Yours, daddy. Please cum on this pussy!"

When she said that, he couldn't help but bust inside of her. She felt him cum and relaxed. She was glad he was finished because her pussy was hurting.

"Damn, girl, you tryna make sure a nigga come back, aren't you."

"Yep," she said while giving him a kiss. "And you tryna make sure I don't leave."

"Yep," he said while laughing.

"I like you. Can we keep this going on for a little while?" she asked. She walked up to him and wrapped her arms around him.

"Let's see where this goes." He was cut short by his phone. "Hello? What up, gangsta?"

"Nigga, where the fuck you at? We have been calling you all day. Felony got shot. They hit up your crib earlier and he got hit in the leg, arm, and stomach saving Lexi and Lovey!" Illy yelled through the phone.

"Where y'all at? I'm on my way," said Kilo.

"We at University Hospital."

"Alright." He hung up. "Put your number in my phone. I gotta go. Some shit just happened."

"I know; I heard." She put her number in his phone, then gave him his gun. "You better call!"

He put on his clothes and went to wake Slugga up.

"Come on. Felony in the hospital."

By the time they were in the truck, Kilo was explaining everything as he sped down I-35.

When they got to the hospital. Illy was outside smoking a cigarette. Before they could even park. Illy was at the truck rushing them to get out.

"What's up? Is he alright? Is he gon' make it or not?" asked Kilo.

"Just come see for y'all selves."

Once they made it inside, he saw that the whole squad was there. Lexi ran up to Kilo and hugged him while crying

"I tried calling you, but you didn't answer," she said, sobbing on his chest.

"It's okay. Can we go in?"

"Yeah."

"Are you good? You didn't get hurt, did you? Whoever did this gon' get theirs fo' sho'," Kilo expressed.

"Yeah, I'm good. Just make sure you stay out of trouble because we need you out here," she said hoping he would catch on.

"I got you. Just let me talk to my homie."

He walked into the room. He and Slugga went in and saw Felony hooked up to all kinds of cords. It hurt him to see his nigga like that. He walked up to him then looked at him. It seemed like Felony felt his presence than opened his eyes.

"What's up, nigga? You just gon' stand there looking like you wanna cry?" Felony said in a low whisper.

"What up, gangsta? I'm glad you made it. I owe you my life, my nigga. If it wasn't for you, Lexi would be gone," he said with tears in my eyes.

"I was on my way to tell you about that nigga you put me on."

"Just chill, my nigga. Don't worry about that no more. Did you see who did this?" asked Slugga.

"Them Block Boy niggas."

"Alright, on everything, I got you. I heard you popped one of them bitch-ass niggas," said Kilo. Felony just laughed softly. "Just get some rest, and thanks for saving Lexi and Lovey."

"No problem and tell them I said when I come home to smoke some more of that fire-ass weed with me."

Everybody laughed at the same time then walked out of the door. It seemed like everybody was looking at Kilo when he walked out, so everybody saw the anger in his eyes. Lexi saw that look and decided to tell him she was pregnant.

"Kilo, let me talk to you," she said, pulling him to the side.

"What's up, half-breed?"

"I know you mad at what happened with Felony and all, but I don't want you doin' anything stupid to end up in jail."

"What you saying? You just expect me to just sit around while my nigga layed up in this bitch with cords and shit on his arm?" he said with hostility in his voice.

"No, I'm not saying that. I just need you to help take care of our baby because I can't do it by myself!" she yelled.

As soon as she said it, everybody turned and looked at Babygurl, including him. All she could do was put her head down because she didn't want nobody to see the hurt.

"Let me handle my business first, then we gon' talk. Can you and Lisa stay with Lovey until we get things straight?" he asked Lexi.

"Yeah. But make sure you come home tonight."

"Alright, and Felony said when he come home have some more of that weed to smoke," he said while smiling.

"Okay," she said with a smile.

They walked back to where everybody was and he asked everybody to meet up at his spot in one hour.

"Lovey, so y'all have a ride home?" asked Kilo.

"I'll call Correy. He'll pick us up."

"Cool."

Kilo and Slugga kissed Lexi and Lisa then walked to the truck.

***

Kilo, Slugga, Illy, Low-Key, and Babygurl all sat in Kilo's living room loading up guns. You could tell everybody's minds were on getting revenge for Felony because the whole room was quiet.

93

"Look, these bitch-ass niggas got a spot-on East Carson and Pine Street. It should be easy to get at 'em because they right on the corner," Babygurl said, breaking the silence.

Kilo heard what Babygurl was saying, but at the same time, his mind was on Lexi. If it wasn't for Felony, Lexi and his baby would be dead. He had got caught slipping and he was fucked up about it, so he planned on getting rid of anybody who got in his way.

"Okay, it's 8:00 p.m. They should be good and set right now. We gon' take my truck and Low-key's ride. Soon as we see it's clear to let them have it, we let loose on the whole house," Kilo said, making sure everybody got what he was saying.

Kilo got up and walked to the back room. Everybody knew that he needed to be alone, so they let him be.

"Babygurl, let me holla at you in the kitchen," Low-key said, walking towards the kitchen.

"What up, kinfolk?" she asked.

"I see those looks you keep giving Kilo. Take it easy on him. He's going through some shit right now."

"What you mean? Look, I'm just here out of respect for Kilo and Felony. Fuck that bitch. And Kilo will hear from me when this is over." She wanted to say more, but she knew what Low-key said was true. She was hurt that Kilo got Lexi pregnant and not her.

"Alright, Babygurl and Illy, y'all ride with me, and Slugga, you ride with Low-key," Kilo said as they were walking outside.

He hopped in his truck and turned up his music. Li'l Boosie's "Mind of Maniac" was playing over and over as Kilo's mind was on Felony. Illy and Babygurl were also quiet because their minds were on the same thing. He was exiting Pine when she started explaining to him what the house looked like. He looked through the rearview mirror to see if Low-key and Slugga were still behind them. When he saw them, he pulled over in an empty parking lot to explain what he needed everybody to do.

"When we get to Carson, I need y'all to park on the side. Just in case them niggas try to run. Everybody must die for my nigga."

After everything was explained, they got back in their rides and drove off. He didn't turn the music back up because he wanted it quiet.

Kilo pulled across the street from the house and Low-key parked on the side. Nobody was outside, but the inside was jumping. As if on cue, three niggas walked out and stood on the porch smoking and drinking.

"Oh, niggas think shit sweet," Illy said, cocking back his Uzi.

At the same time, Kilo pulled out two twin 40's and Babygurl had her 9mm on her lap with two extra clips. Illy stepped out the back of the truck and yelled to the group of niggas.

"Hey, what's up with one of them whole thangs, gangsta?"

"Nigga, get the fuck from in front my trap!" one nigga yelled.

He never saw the Uzi behind Illy's back or Low-key and Slugga creeping up on the side of the house. Illy never responded back to him as he came from behind his back and let the Uzi go. Before the nigga that was popping of at the mouth could dive out of the way, bullets riddled him and he shook to the ground. Kilo came from behind the truck and dumped on the other two niggas but was too late because they had already crawled inside. Kilo, Illy, and Babygurl took off towards the

95

trap and heard the pump that Low-key had let loose. When he heard that, he knew they were tryna get away. Babygurl was the first one through the door and hit one in the head and chest, dropping him instantly.

"Babygurl, fall back!" Kilo yelled. He didn't want her to get hurt.

Kilo heard noises coming from the kitchen and started off towards it. He saw someone behind the refrigerator and let off a shot off to his leg and he fell. When he saw that it was one of them niggas, he stood over him. "Bitch-ass nigga! I hope shooting my homie made y'all feel good, because he the reason you died." He shot him four times in the face, kicked him, and the walked off. He made it to the hallway and the squad was there waiting.

"That might be everybody," Slugga said.

When he said that, they heard a noise come from the backroom. Low-key and Babygurl dashed towards the back with theirs gun out. They got to the back and she saw somebody trying to get out of the window. She ran up on him and stuck her 9mm between his ass cheeks.

"If you move or even tighten up yo' ass cheeks, I'ma blow 'em off!" she said. "Get yo' bitch ass down, tryna run and shit." When he got down, she pushed him in the living room and made him sit down on the couch.

"Alright gangsta, I'ma give you a chance to live. Where is the money?" Kilo told the homie.

"Fuck you! You gon' kill me anyways, so you might as well get it over so I can see yo' weak-ass homeboy where I'm going," he said with a grin on his face. Before Kilo could say something Slugga and Low-key emptied their guns into him.

"I guess we gotta tear this bitch up then. Get whateva looks like money so we can bounce," Kilo said, walking out of the door a minute before the police showed up.

Ray Vinci

Chapter 15

Detective Stronbone just pulled up to the house and could see it was gon' be a hell of a case. The house looked like Swiss cheese so whoever did this was trying to tear down the whole house. He stepped out of the car and started walking towards the house. Detective Stronbone was 6'5" and weighed about 250 pounds. He was white with dirty blonde hair. Everybody knew what he was about. If he could pin a body or dope on you just to get a case, he would do it.

Before he made it to the house, a local cop that was working the scene filled him in on everything that was going on.

Stronbone stepped inside and the smell of gunpowder, blood, and bleach hit his nose, making him gag. He knew by the bleach being poured everywhere that he wasn't going to be able get any fingerprints.

"So, what do you git for me?" he asked the ME.

"We got six bodies: one on the porch, one on the kitchen, one right here, and three in the back," said the ME. He pulled the sheet off of the body that was the couch. When he saw what happened to that body, he instantly thought about what happened to that kid Rico. He pulled the sheet back over and stood up. He had a feeling that both of these murders were done by the same people.

He walked through the house and collected all the evidence he could. There were several different types of bullets in the house. He collected them all, then gave them to a local to send to forensics for testing. He also found guns in the back room. He passed those guns and bullets off to get bullets tested too.

"Get those guns and bullets checked out and get 'em back to me ASAP," he told the local cop.

"Okay, I'll have something for you in a couple of days."

He was about to walk up front when he heard his name being called.

"Detective Stronbone!" The voice was coming from the living room.

When he got up front, he saw who was calling him. It was his partner, Detective Reyes.

"I just got a call that said the victim from yesterday afternoon just woke up. He's at University Hospital."

"Okay, let's take a ride and see what we can find out.

***

Kilo was on his way to pick up Lexi. His music was turned up loud, but he was still in a zone. He was snapped out of his zone when he heard horns honking. He forgot he was stopped at a red light, so he hit the gas and burned off. Before he got to the next block, his phone started ringing. Usher's "There Goes My Baby" started playing and he knew it was Babygurl texting him. He opened up the text and read that she needed to talk to him. He texted back and told her he would stop by at 6:00 p.m.

When he pulled into Spring Hill, everybody seemed to be moving at once. He was driving through the apartments slowly when he saw Lexi and Lovey walking back towards the apartment. He could tell something was wrong by the looks on their faces. He was pulling up on them when he saw a group of niggas following them and talking shit. Kilo rolled up on them and rolled the window down.

"What's up, half-breed, y'all good?" he asked with his hand on his 40 cal.

"Yeah, we cool, it ain't nothing," she said, rushing to the truck because she knew how Kilo was when it came to her well-being.

"It ain't none of yo' business, nigga, so move the fuck on while we holla at these fine-ass bitches!" one nigga said while licking his lips and grabbing his nuts.

Kilo got pissed off and parked the truck, then hung his right hand out of the window. "Say, bitch-ass nigga, watch yo' fucking mouth before I heat that bitch up. And watch how you talk to my li'l mama before I smoke you and ya homies!" he said while exposing his strap.

"Come on, Chucky, let's go," another one said.

"Smart choice, homie," Kilo said with a smirk on his face. He pulled up in front of the apartment, parked, and got out. "What's up, baby?" He hugged Lexi. "What's up, Lovey, you cool?"

"Yeah, I'm good. Where the weed at? I know you got that fire."

"Damn, is that all y'all do is smoke?" he asked sarcastically. "I got some in the truck. Roll up. You might as well smoke all you can today because this yo' last day."

A big smile came across her face because all she wanted was for Kilo to be happy.

When Lovey made it back she gave one to Lexi and she kept one as they both lit up. All three were chilling so hard that they didn't even see Correy pull up. Kilo turned around quick when he saw it was Correy and then went into their stare down. This time it was a stare of recognition.

"Well, we gotta go. I'ma catch up with you tonight," Lexi told her sister.

"Okay, call me."

When they got out of the truck, she put the playlist on Tre Songz and peeled off.

"So, what you got planned? I hope it's some food, because this baby and this weed got a bitch hungry."

Kilo just smiled because Lexi looked sexy when she was high and she had a glow. He was thinking about when she first approached him when she snapped him out of his thoughts.

"Baby, we getting pulled over."

He looked in the rearview mirror and saw who it was and knew there was something wrong. He tucked his gun and weed, then waited for them to come. Detective Stronbone was on his way, so Kilo rolled down the window.

"Well, well, well, if it ain't Mr. Kilo himself."

"What's up, Detective, how can I help you?" Kilo asked Stronbone.

"I want to ask you a few questions."

"Shoot," said Kilo

"How long have you been out? About a year now?" Stronbone estimated.

"Yeah, and ya point is?" replied Kilo in slick tone.

"Tell me what you know about these robbings and killings going on. I know that's your line of work."

"I don't know shit. I'm legit. I'm out of the business," Kilo said, sounding aggravated.

"Well, I know your homeboy got shot up in front of your house and saved that pretty lady of yours right there." Stronbone said. "I know it's a matter of time before you retaliate, if you haven't already. Just know this time."

Kilo smirked and was about to say something smart, but his partner called him to go back the station.

"Next time I see you; your ass is going to jail for aggravated robbery and capital murder. So you better lawyer up, boy," he said, then walked back to his car. When Stronbone pulled off he waited for a while, then pulled off into traffic.

***

Correy had just left the house to go pick Quick up from the trap so they could pick up some more work from Philly. The apartments where the trap was ended up being a gold mine. The work was going fast, plus Keisha was bringing in money too. He had to get some more work before 9:00 p.m. tonight because that's when it started pumping the most. He looked at his phone to see that it was 5:30 p.m., so he had enough time to get everything in order.

As he got to Rittman and I-35, he glanced to his right. He thought he saw someone who looked familiar but couldn't pin the face on anyone. The Mexican girl driving the car looked so familiar too. Then it popped in his head. He last saw Rico with a Mexican girl. Murder instantly became his number one priority. He turned around and made his way into the Exxon station. By the time he made it there, she was already pulling off, so he jumped behind her and followed her.

He wasn't sure if it was her, but he sure was about to find out. He got on the freeway going towards the east side. He clutched his strap because if it was her, he was gon' blow her head off the first chance he got. He knew he had better shit to do, but Rico was like a brother to him, and he made a promise to himself to kill whoever did it.

She zoomed past the green light that had just turned red and made him stop.

"Shit!" he yelled out loud. He thought to himself about what he was gon' do if it was her and smiled to himself. The light turned green and smashed on the gas pedal hard. When he sped off, the police on a side road jumped behind him and hit their lights.

When he realized he was getting pulled over, he hit a few corners to try and throw the pistol he had. The police were right behind him every block he hit, so he never had a chance to throw the strap. He realized that he was not about to get away. He pulled over and prepared to go to jail. He lit a cigarette, then waited for the officer to walk up.

Chapter 16

Babygurl had just pulled into the driveway of her house. She was expecting Low-key to be here, but he wasn't. She lit up a Sweet because she was nervous. She could have sworn somebody was following her. If she hadn't sped past that light before it turned red, he would have caught up to her.

When she was getting out of the car, she got a text from Kilo that said he was on his way. She intended to let Kilo know just how she felt about everything that was going on between them. She went inside and rolled up some more weed. After she rolled up the weed, she jumped in the shower. It took her fifteen minutes to shower. While she was drying off, she heard a knock on the door. She wrapped a towel around her body and then went to open the door. When she looked through the peephole and saw Kilo, she opened it.

"Damn, what took you so long to answer the door? You got a nigga in this bitch or something?" Kilo asked, joking.

"I just might. What you worried about it for?"

"Alright, don't get nobody smoked by playing and shit."

"Whateva. It's some blunts on the table. Light up while I go put some clothes on," she said while walking away.

Kilo turned around and he could see her ass jiggle through the towel. "Damn that ass still fat," he said to himself.

He sat on the couch, lit a blunt then turned on the TV. He put in "Baby Boy", then sat back and waited for Babygurl to come back. When she walked back in, she had on his old pair of boxers and old muscle T-shirt.

"I see you keep old shit," he said while looking her up and down.

"Yeah, something like that," she said. "So, I guess you have a baby now?"

"Yeah, my bad if I hurt you by it, but shit just happened," Kilo said hitting the blunt.

"So, what's up, what's gon' happen with us?"

"Shit, you gon' always be my Babygurl, but you gon' have to accept the fact that me and Lexi together. I know you might not like it, but I expect you to be somewhat happy."

It took a few seconds to digest what he was saying. She inhaled some smoke and then passed the blunt to him.

"I'm happy for you, but don't expect me to be nice to that bitch. I need to ask you a question."

"Shoot."

"Can a bitch still get some dick from time to time?"

All Kilo could do was smile. He reached over grabbed her and starting kissing her.

***

It was 11:00 p.m. at night when Kilo walked out of Baby-gurl's house. His phone vibrated, indicating he had a text message. When he saw that it was Slugga, he called instead of texting back.

"What up wit' it gangsta?" he said while getting in his truck.

"I'm at the hospital and the laws been snooping around all day," Slugga said.

"I know. That pussy-ass Stronbone pulled me over early talkin' about what happened."

"Oh yeah, nigga caught me while I was coming to visit Felony."

"I'ma be up there in the morning. I'm about to skate to Illy's crib. I'ma hit you up later," said Kilo.

"Alright. Bianca said hit her up," he said, then hung up.

Kilo started up his truck and pulled off. He started to call Lexi to let her know he was going to his brother's house but decided to do it later.

He got on the freeway and turned up his music. He thought about how close he came to going to jail while Lexi was with him. He was so into his thoughts that when he tried to switch lanes, he almost crashed into another car. When the person blew his horn, Kilo saw that it was Illy signaling him to exit Kilo sped up and followed him. He got off on White at the Exxon and pulled into the gas station. Illy rode up on the side of him and Kilo realized he had somebody in the car with him. He jumped out of his truck and gave his li'l bro some dap.

"What's up, gangsta, who that you got wit' you?"

"Oh, that's my nigga Tre. Today his G-day so we finna hit up Paradise. You tryna roll wit' us or what?" said Illy.

"I was just on my way to yo' shit anyways. Let me go get some cigarettes and gas." He went inside the store.

When Kilo got back, Illy and Tre were slap-boxing on the side of the car. From the looks of it, Tre was giving Illy a run for his money, but he knew Illy would easily lay hands on him.

Kilo filled up his tank and told Illy to follow him. Before they pulled off, he rolled down his window and turned up his music. When Jeezy started bumping, everybody's eyes were on Kilo as he swung out of the store.

When they pulled up to Paradise, the parking lot was full of bad-ass bitches and nigga looks like they had money. He parked and Illy and Tre walked up smoking a Sweet. Kilo left his banger because he came to spend some money, not trip. They got in with no problem and went to drop some cash.

Kilo, Illy, and Tre headed to the bar and ordered a bottle of Ciroc, then went to the back of the club. As soon as they sat down, a yellow bone stripper that look like Stacey Dash and had an ass like Melissa Ford started bouncing her ass to 2 Chains's version of "Back That Ass Up". Tre instantly started dropping 20's on her and Kilo and Illy followed suit because baby was doing her thing. She drew a crowd, but she was paying attention to Illy. She motioned for Illy to meet her in the back and he nodded to let Kilo know what was up. As he sat down next to Tre, a white girl with an ass like a horse walked by. Kilo couldn't help but stop her.

"Whoa! Hold up li'l mama, slow down and kick it with ya' boy."

"Boy, what I look like, one of these strippers up in here?" she said, trying to sound black, but her white side wouldn't let her.

"Naw, that's why I stopped you. Who you here with?" he asked.

"I'm here with my friends."

Kilo instantly started looking around to see who she was talking about. When he saw who she was talking about, he shook his head. Right when he turned around to talk to li'l mama, he saw someone he knew out the corner of his eye. She was beautiful in her business pant suit and he could tell she had ass. He noticed she was talking to some guy. As he stared, ole girl left and Illy came back to chill. Kilo was tipsy and it was damn near 3:00 a.m., so he decided to take things home. They were headed to the door when Bianca and Valerie and their homegirl approached them.

"So, you just gon' leave without saying anything to me?" asked Bianca.

"Oh, my bad, I thought that was yo' man you was talking to earlier," Kilo said.

"Hell naw! He wish he could hit this. What's up, can we kick it for a minute?" she asked Kilo.

"Yeah. Let's go outside and smoke something."

They all walked to his truck and smoked a couple if Sweets while Kilo and Bianca talked. He told her he had to leave but promised to call her since he hadn't done so in the past two weeks.

Ray Vinci

Chapter 17

Kilo and Lexi jumped out of their sleep to someone banging on the front door. Lexi got out of bed and went to answer it, the Kilo got out of bed five minutes later since Lexi didn't come back. He walked in the living room to Lovey crying like she lost her best friend. Instead of getting involved, he went to the kitchen to return a couple of calls. The first call was to Slugga to let him know he was on his way to the hospital in a couple of hours. The second call was to Illy to see if he got home okay.

When he walked back in the living room, Lovey had calmed down. He lit up a Newport then sat next to Lexi as they explained what happened to Correy. He really didn't care but he didn't show it. Instead, he comforted her.

"Say, I'm finna ride to the hospital to check on Felony. If y'all wanna go, y'all can," said Kilo.

"Yeah, we gon' go, but can you take her to go see Correy?" said Lexi.

"Yeah, but pull yo' car in the driveway," he told Lovey.

Lovey went to pull her car in the driveway while Lexi and Kilo went to get dressed.

Kilo was dressed regular in some black cargo shorts, a grey Tony Parker San Antonio Spurs Jersey, a black Spurs snap-back, and some grey and black Retro 8's. They all got in his truck then drove to go see Felony.

***

Detective Stronbone had just received a phone call from Detective Reyes that the same bullets that were found in the house were the same ones found in the kid that was laid up in the hospital. He was on his way to the hospital to question the victim. He knew that Kilo had something to do with the murders because some of the bullets matched the ones in Rico's body. He pulled up to the front and a big smile came across his face because he just saw Kilo walk inside. He parked his car and walked up to Felony's room. When he got to the room, it was full of people, but he walked in anyways.

"Well, what do we got going on in here?" he asked.

Everybody looks at the door because they all recognized his voice.

"Damn, what do you want? Can't you see we having a family moment?" Kilo asked with aggravation in his voice.

"I'm family, ain't I?" he said be sarcastic. "I'm here to question your homeboy over there."

"I ain't answering shit! Fuck you!" Felony said.

"Have it your way, but you and your boy Kilo are going down when I find out he's responsible for Rico's murder, and what happened in the house. As a matter of fact, I can haul Kilo in with the information I got on his black ass."

Kilo was so mad that he could see the heat in his eyes. He wanted to charge at Stronbone, but he played his cards right.

"If you not here to arrest nobody, then you need to leave." Kilo said, trying to stay calm.

Slugga, Illy, Low-Key, Lexi, and Lovey all looked at Kilo and Stronbone like they were two boxers fighting for a championship title.

"I will, but I will be back to take his ass to jail for murder when I do find out," he said, pointing at Felony and then walking out of the door.

Everybody was quiet when he left. Illy was the first one to break the silence.

112

"Don't worry, gangsta, we gon' get you a top-notch lawyer after we hit this lick tonight."

"Thanks," was all he could say while holding his head down.

Lexi went over to comfort him because she knew he was in need of it.

Kilo was lost in his thoughts, trying to figure out how he got caught. Or was he just bluffing to see how he would react to what he was saying? He really didn't want to take any chances hitting any licks, but he had to get Felony a lawyer. He owed him that much.

"Lexi, Lovey, y'all take the truck and go see ya boy. I'ma ride with Illy," he told Lexi. He gave her some money and the keys.

"Okay, call me if anything happens." She gave Kilo a kiss and then walked out.

Kilo and his squad stayed at the hospital a little bit longer. Felony let them know that he would be released from the hospital soon and to hurry up. Kilo rode with Illy and Slugga left with Low-Key.

"You need to get rid of that burner and cop a new one," Illy said while looking at the road.

"I know, but before we do what we gotta do tonight, I'ma get two twin Desert Eagles," said Kilo. "So, where we gon' be hitting this lick at?"

"I know a couple of niggas over there off Hackberry that be moving some heavy weight, so their money right. I got some niggas on standby waiting on some bricks so we good on that."

"Alright. I guess you run point on this one and I'm gon' back you up. Just make sure everything go right."

***

When Lexi and Lovey pulled up to the county jail. She couldn't help but think about what Detective Stronbone was saying to Kilo. She didn't want to be coming to see Kilo in jail, especially while she was pregnant. She knew he was in the streets, but she didn't know he was that deep. Lovey was yelling at her, which made her snap out of her thoughts.

"You gon' wait in line with me, or you gon' sit here?" Lovey asked Lexi.

"I'ma wait in line with you."

When they walked to the door, the line was long, but it seemed to be moving fast. It took Lovey thirty minutes to get to the visiting booth and she was pissed. Correy walked up with a smile on his face and her mood seemed to change.

"What's up, why you looking like a bum?" Correy asked from behind the glass partition that was between them.

"'Cause you in jail and a bitch been crying all night. So, what they got you for?"

"A pistol case. I don't know how long I'ma be in this bitch."

"Do you got a bond? I can get you out," she said while digging in her bag for some money.

"Yeah, but I'd rather sit this one out. I'll only be in here for a month or two and then I'm gon' be out," he guessed, while trying to offer her hope.

"I can't wait that long, baby. I need you out here with me," she said with tears in her eyes.

"Girl, stop crying. You good, so chill out."

"I might move in with Lexi or let Lisa move in with me."

"Cool. What's up wit' Quick? Have you talked to him?"

"Naw, but I'll let him know to come visit, so put him on yo' list."

"Is it cool if he stay with you? I'ma tell him to hit you with some bread for the bills."

"It's cool, but he ain't having that bitch stay with him," she said with an attitude.

The chopped it up for a while and she felt a lot better than before. She walked outside and spotted Lexi sitting in the truck, talking on her phone.

"Look, Kilo, I'm not gon' sit up here and pretend like I don't care what you do. You need to get yo' shit together!" she yelled through the phone.

"You knew what you was getting into before we started this. If you having second thoughts, you need to let me know. Bring my truck so I can handle my business!"

She had pissed him of, but she wasn't going through this shit with him. She said nothing to Lovey and just drove off.

Ray Vinci

Chapter 18

Kilo was mad as hell. He stood on his porch, waiting on Lexi to pull up with his truck while smoking a Newport. He couldn't believe how Lexi was acting. He thought she would hold him down through whatever. He threw the butt of the cigarette and lit another one. He was wondering what was taking her so long. Right when he was about to call her, he spotted her coming down the street. When she pulled up to the driveway, he almost ran up to the truck. Kilo tried to say something to her, but she just walked straight into the house. He was about to go after her, but he already tried to talk, so he just jumped in his truck and peeled off. Once he got down the street, his phone started to ring. He started to let it go because he thought it was less, but when he saw it was Crazy C, he answered.

"What's up, gangsta? Talk to me. You ready for me or what?" Kilo asked

"Yeah. Meet me at Spanish Oak Apartments on Harry Wusbach back in fifteen minutes." Crazy C said and then hung up.

Kilo jumped on I-10 and rode in silence. When he realized he was about to pass up the exit, he crossed all four lanes without using his signal. The whole time he was driving, he never saw the Detective Stronbone and his partner following him. He got off on Harry Wusbach and turned into the gas station to get some gas and Newports. Before he walked in the store, he got a text from Crazy C asking where he was. He texted him back and told him to meet him at the gas station down the street. As he pumped his gas, he noticed Crazy C's royal blue

Bonneville one blades. Before Crazy C could get out, Kilo was in the passenger seat. When he got in, he showed him twin Desert Eagles. All Kilo could do was smile. For one, he wasn't naked anymore, and for two, they were just his style.

"They gon' run you $200 apiece. They both clean, plus the numbers scratched off," Said Crazy C.

"I ain't tripping," Kilo said while counting $400 out of his wad of cash. When the deal was made, Kilo put the guns back in the backpack then got out of the car. As he made it back to his truck, he noticed a group of young niggas looking and pointing at his truck.

Kilo looked at the group a second time and realized he knew them from somewhere. He finally registered that they were the same niggas he, Slugga, and Illy had to rough up behind Lisa. Before he could reach for the straps in his backpack, shots were already being fired in his direction. Kilo dove behind his truck, then took out his twins. When he came from around the truck, the whole crew was walking towards the truck slowly, so he took his chance and let loose on them. One of them saw Kilo move and let the other two know that he had his straps out.

All three of them were able to get out of the way of the gunfire that was raining down on them. The one that Kilo hit when that incident went down over Lisa seemed to get up and start moving his way, and the other two seemed to stay on the ground. Kilo ducked behind the truck, then waited for him to come around. As soon as he rounded the truck, Kilo was already on him with both Desert Eagles pointed at his head.

"Bitch-ass nigga, you just made yo' worst mistake!" Kilo said through clenched teeth. Before he could squeeze the trigger, he heard a familiar voice.

"Freeze!" Detective Stronbone yelled while easing up on Kilo slowly. "Put the guns down and back away from him!"

Kilo had no choice and put the guns down, then he backed up. They put them in handcuffs and waited for back up. Kilo sat next to the police car with his head down, wondering how he got caught slipping.

"Looks like I finally got your black ass."

"Fuck you, pig-ass bitch," he said with aggressiveness in his voice.

While Kilo waited to get escorted to jail, all he could think about was Lexi.

***

Lisa had just walked in the house. The sun was going down and the house was quiet. As soon as she started turning around, Lexi came from the back. Lisa could tell she was crying because her nose and eyes were red.

"Girl, what's wrong with you? I've been trying to call you for five hours," Lisa said with concern in her voice.

Lexi walked to the couch and sat down. She didn't want to put her problems on anybody else, but she needed somebody to talk to.

"I turned my phone off because me and Kilo got into it and he hasn't come home yet," she said with tears flowing from her eyes.

"It's gonna be all right. He's just going through a lot with you being pregnant and Felony in the hospital. Plus that detective that's always popping up out of nowhere," Lisa explained. "You know what? I got something to ease the pain." Lisa reached in her purse and pulled out a Sweet.

They lit it up. She started to tell her sister no, but she needed something to take the feeling away. They talked about how she felt about Kilo being in the streets.

"Bitch, you know what you were getting into when you get with him. Before you sign the contract, you better read the fine print."

"Damn, bitch, you either been talking to that nigga Kilo or you feeling the shit out of that weed, because you damn near said what he said," Lexi said, stealing the weed.

It was quiet because she was thinking about what Lisa was telling her. She knew Kilo had been in the streets since they were young. Kilo was her world and now that she finally had him, she might lose him. Without saying anything, she jumped up to get her cell phone to call Kilo. When she got to her phone and turned it on, she had a bunch of missed calls. When she called it back, it couldn't go through. She tried Slugga and it went straight to voicemail and Illy's did the same. She went to the living room and Lisa was on the phone talking to Slugga.

"Yeah, she's here," Lisa said.

"I'm on my way right now. Stay there and I'll explain everything when I get there."

"What was that about?" asked Lexi.

"I don't know. He said he'll explain when he gets here. What's wrong with you?"

"Kilo's not answering his phone."

"He'll be back tonight. Just chill."

Lisa had gotten Lexie to chill while they puffed on another blunt. It seemed like as soon as she started feeling the weed, somebody started knocking like they were the damn police. When she opened the door, it was Slugga and Illy.

"Where is Kilo at, and why y'all like you just lost your best friend?" she asked.

"Look, Lexi, Kilo just got locked up for a shootout on Harry Wusbach," Illy said.

Lexi's whole face turned pale as she started crying. "It's my fault. We got into it and he tried to talk to me, but I didn't want to hear it."

"It's okay, Lexi, he gonna be all right. When they give him a bond, we go get him out," said Lisa.

Lexi calmed down and then went to sleep after they promised to take her to Kilo tomorrow.

Ray Vinci

Chapter 19

Correy sat in front of the TV watching the 12 p.m. news when he heard the doors to the tank slide open. He didn't pay any attention to it because he was in his own zone. If it wasn't for his spades partner calling him for the next game, he would have never turned around.

"Damn, nigga, you gon' come win some bread or you gon' stand there looking like a bum?" Ray Ray said

"Yeah, I just thought I saw somebody I knew," Correy responded.

I know that ain't that nigga Kilo. I must be tripping, he thought to himself. He started remembering that they had run across each other. It seemed like when he came around, he would mug the shit out of him, but it also was a sense of respect at the same time. He could tell Kilo was a stand-up nigga by the way he carried himself, so he wanted as little beef as possible.

"What you say, nigga? You talking to yourself or what?" his opponent asked.

"Nigga, I said up the bet with yo' broke ass. Two dollar a game playing-ass nigga," Correy said, capping.

"Shit, it don't matter, we can play five dollars a game," he said.

"Fuck it, that probably all you got anyways," Correy shot back.

***

When Kilo walked in, he went straight to his cell to put his things up. He wanted to lay down and pass out because he was tired as hell, but he had to make some calls. Before he could make it down the stairs, he heard a familiar voice, but couldn't place it so he paid it no mind. When he made it to where the phones were, they were occupied, so he waited. While he was waiting, somebody tapped him on his shoulder.

"What's up, ugly-ass nigga?"

Kilo turned around and saw his homie. He couldn't help but smile.

"Loksta, my nigga, what up, gangster?" Kilo asked with a big-ass smile on his face. He was happy to see a familiar face while he was in here.

"Nothing, just waiting til these few weeks pass so I can dip out this bitch."

Loksta was a caramel-complexion and stood at 6'1" and 195 pounds. People thought he was mixed because he had curly hair that hung down to his ears. Loksta was a loyal nigga when it came to ridin', plus everybody was cool with him.

"These hoes got me on——" Kilo quit and finished the sentence because a Mexican got on the phone he was waiting for.

"Say, gangsta, I was waiting on that phone."

"You gon' have to wait some more, homeboy," the Mexican said and then finished dialing.

He laughed to himself because he didn't feel like going through this shit right now, but he was far from a hoe. "Say, gangsta," he said as he tapped him on the shoulder. "I told you I was waiting on that phone."

"And I told you to wait some more, nigga!" He turned around and got in Kilo's face.

Seeing this happen and knowing Kilo's attitude, Loksta stepped in between them. Out of the corner of his eye, he saw the whole day room stand up, but one face stood out the most. When Correy came his way, he thought he was going to have to whip his ass too.

"What up, Joe, everything good?" Correy asked.

"Yeah, I'm good, you good?" he shot back.

"It ain't even like that this way, Joe. I'm trying to see if you good on this situation right here."

Before Kilo could explain the Mexican reached across Loksta and punched Kilo on the side of his head.

Knowing that the fight was about to get ugly. Loksta stepped out of the way. Just as he stepped aside, the Mexican rushed him and tried to hit him with a wild punch that Kilo easily side-stepped. Kilo was ready, posted up, when he saw Correy talking to one of the Mexicans. He stepped in and hit him twice in the nose and instantly made him grab his face.

With no hesitation, he hit him with a right hook that stumbled him, almost knocking him down. With how hard Kilo hit him, he should think about backing down, but he didn't. The Mexican rushed him with his head down, swinging wild punches. Kilo started backpedaling, connecting uppercuts on every inch of his face. The Mexican instantly stopped swinging and grabbed Kilo by the waist. He slipped his leg on the side of Kilo's, then slung him to the ground.

"Alright, alright, that's enough!" said the one Correy was talking to.

Correy pulled them apart, then helped Kilo off the ground. He couldn't help but stare at the Mexican Correy was talking once he got up. He gave Kilo a head nod and then walked off with the rest of his homeboys.

"You good, Kilo?" Loksta asked.

"I'm straight," he said, looking at Correy at the same time. "Thanks for having my back, homie."

"No problem. Call me when you get yaself together," he said and then walked off.

Kilo wasn't even in the mood to use the phone anymore and wanted to chill out.

"Say, I'm finna go lay down. Hit me if something shakes," he told Loksta and then burned off.

When he got to his cell, his celly was sitting in his bunk. He wasn't gon' say nothing to him until he saw it was an old school cat.

"What up, O.G?" said Kilo.

"Looks like you ain't no stranger to holding ya own, so if you need anything, let me know," he said.

"Alright," Kilo said while he grabbed his clothes then left.

***

When Kilo woke up, it was 9:00 a.m., and it felt like he had been asleep for ages.

"Youngsta, I've been tryna wake you up for five minutes now. They've been calling you for an attorney visit," his celly, Mr. Lee, said.

Kilo realized that Mr. Lee stood at 6'2" and 225 pounds of pure muscle. He was bald-headed with light skin and a full beard and mustache cut low.

Kilo jumped up to brush his teeth and put on his clothes. As soon as he was done, he dashed out of the cell. There were only a couple of niggas in the dayroom, but they all acknowledged him as he left the tank. It took him a few minutes to get to the visitation booth, but it seemed like he was waiting forever. He remember when he was told he was getting a court appointed lawyer. When he saw who appeared in front of him. His mouth dropped open because he was surprised.

"Hey, Mr. Johnson, I'm going to be your lawyer on this case," Bianca said while smiling at him.

"I didn't know you was a lawyer. How did you know I was here?"

"Your friends called me to let me know." She winked at him. "You're here on Agg. Assault with a deadly weapon. Explain to me what happened."

Kilo told her everything from start to finish, and the whole time he was talking, she was smiling.

"Okay, I can help you because it was self-defense. I wish I could stay a little while longer, but I gotta go see another client. Here's my number. Call me as soon as you can."

She blew him a kiss and a "call me" sign, then walked off.

Ray Vinci

Chapter 20

Quick had just finished cooking up the last brick he had when he stepped outside. The trap him and Correy had before he got locked up was doing numbers. He was moving nine zones a day and it looks like it was picking up. Correy had connected Quick with Philly so they could link up every time he needed some more work. Every chance he got he was dropping bread on Correy's books, putting food in the house, and paying bills. The money was coming faster than he thought. He now owned a blue CTS on 3 bar blades with a stereo system that could be heard three blocks away.

He had just lit up a Newport when a red Mustang pulled up in front of the apartment. When he saw that it was his boy Tre, he knew it was all good, but when he saw somebody else in the passenger seat, he started trying to see who it was. Tre got out of the car walked up to show Quick some love.

"What up, nigga? Why you looking like that and shit?" asked Tre.

"Who that you got with you?" Quick asked.

"Oh, that's my nigga, Illy. He alright. He good people. What the money looking like?"

Quick had known Tre forever so he decided to put him down with some work, plus he needed some help with the spot since it was jumping extra hard.

"It's jumpin'. I'm waiting on Keisha to come and cop a four and a baby right now." Keisha had her own thing going on another side of town and was copping a big chunk of work he was moving.

"Well, let me get a couple of zones off of you right now."

Ray Vinci

"All right, come here." he said, walking towards the door. "And tell your homie to come in so the law won't just see him sitting here."

Tre waved at Illy and told him to come in and then walked inside. Quick was just pulling the work out of his stash when Illy walked in. He looked him up and down, trying to get a feel of him.

"What up gangsta?" he said while giving Illy dap.

"Quick, is it cool if I chill and make a couple of dollars?" asked Tre.

"Ain't trippin', nigga, but my li'l mama coming to make some ends too, so we gon' have to bust down three ways."

"Cool, I just need to make up for what I lost in the strip club the other night." He and Illy laughed at the same time.

"Say nigga, put in the game so I can wax that ass!" said Tre.

"If it ain't a $100 bet, I ain't playing," Quick boasted. "Can't nobody fuck with me anyway."

"I'll bet you $100 and bet Tre on the side," said Illy.

They both looked at him like he was crazy. When he didn't budge, Quick was the first to say something.

"All right, I got OKC!"

"I got the Spurs!" said Illy.

Tre lit up a blunt as they both stood in front of the TV. Quick was losing by 15 points when he heard a knock on the door. He thought it was a sale, so he told Tre to go get it. Tre opened the door and Keisha walked straight in.

"What's up, baby?" she said while kissing him on the cheek then looking at Illy.

"What's up?" he said but was focused on the game.

"I brought my homegirl with me, is it cool if she kick it?"

"Yeah."

Keisha was loyal to Quick so he looked out for her anytime he could. He knew she was grimy, but that's what he liked about her.

When Keisha's homegirl walked in, everybody stopped and stared at her except Illy. She came in and sat on the couch at the same time Keisha came back.

"Sasha, stop acting all shy and roll up some of that fire-ass loud you got," Keisha said.

When Illy heard the name, he turned to look at her. It looked like she was trying to avoid looking at him, but couldn't.

Instead of worrying about it, he continued playing the game. Illy whipped on Quick and Tre and came up on $400 dollars. Everybody was high as hell, including Sasha, so she started to loosen up around Illy.

"Look out, Tre, I got a dip, my nigga just hit me up," Illy lied trying to see what Sasha was about to do.

"Yeah, I got a dip too," said Quick.

Tre and Illy were the first to leave. Illy told Tre to park down the street. Tre was confused, so Illy ran the story down.

"Just follow the bitch to see where she getting dropped off at."

When Keisha drove past them, Tre hit the lights and pulled right off behind them. It took them ten minutes to get to where Keisha was dropping off Sasha.

"All right, drop me off at my car," said Illy.

***

Illy pulled up to the Artisians off of Benz Engleman. There were only a few people still out. Instead of him pulling up to her apartment, he circled around two times, then parked by the pool. Illy turned the corner to where her apartment was and saw a nigga walk inside. He checked both his 9mm's then started towards the door. When he knocked, he heard footsteps, which made him put his hands behind his back. As the nigga answered the door, Illy clutched both his straps.

"Is Sasha here, homie?" he asked, trying to hide the anger in his voice.

"Yeah, hold up." He yelled back to Sasha, "Aye li'l sis, some nigga here to see you!"

"Okay, I'm coming!" she yelled back.

He had left the door wide open so he saw Sasha coming out of the bathroom in just her bra and panties. Illy couldn't help but think how fine she was. She finally reached the door and when she realized who it was standing there, her eyes got big. Before she could close the door, Illy kicked it back open and walk inside.

"Ahhhh!" Sasha screamed as she tried to run towards the back.

"Naw, bitch, don't scream now!" Illy said. With clenched teeth, he grabbed Sasha by the waist and threw her to the floor.

Illy looked up and saw her brother running out of the room. He didn't realize how big he was until he started running up on him. He pointed both his guns at him and he stopped.

"Act like you wanna do something and I'ma send you home early!" he said while looking him in the eyes.

"Whatever you want, I can give it to you," she said while crying.

"Sasha, what's this about? You know this nigga?!"

"Shut the fuck up, bitch-ass nigga, before I smoke yo' stupid ass. She knows what this is about!" he said as spit flew out of his mouth. Illy felt himself getting pissed off more every time he looked at her.

"I'm sorry, I had no idea what was going on until that happened. I'm sorry," she explained while crying.

He slapped Sasha with the barrel of the gun. When her brother saw what happened, he jumped up and ran towards Illy. Before he could even get to Illy, he shot him in both his knees and he fell.

"Ahhh!" he screamed while grabbing his knees.

"Just tell me where the money is and I'm gone," said Illy.

"It's in the back. Take everything. Just don't kill us, Illy!" she pleaded.

Illy went and got everything that was valuable, then came back up front. "I ought to smoke yo' ass, you dumb bitch." He spit on her as he left.

Ray Vinci

Chapter 21

Correy had just come from his visit with Lovey when he thought he saw a familiar face. He could have sworn that was the nigga Quick said was peeping them at the spot. He didn't know for sure so he shrugged it off and headed back to his tank. On the way back, he was thinking about how Lovey told him that Quick was doing all right with the trap. He began to put a plan together on how to take over the streets and all he needed was a team. As he walked in the tank, he spotted Kilo talking to his old school celly. He remembered that he never had the chance to get up with him since he'd been here, so he made a mental note on that. Correy had to make a call to Quick to catch up on what'd been going on, so he headed straight to the phone.

"Damn, nigga, you calling early?" Quick asked, sounding sleepy.

"Nigga, it's 12:00 p.m., get your ass up," Correy said, laughing. "What's going on out there?" He already knew most of it but he wanted to hear quick version.

"Everything is everything, but I got into it with some off brand niggas saying I'm stepping on they toes," explained Quick.

"Oh yeah, niggas tripping like that? It gots to be doing good out there."

"Yeah, it is, but I might bring it to them niggas if they come through again."

"What, them niggas think something weak 'cause you one deep? Just chill. I'ma get back up. I'm 'bout to be up out this bitch soon." He hung up, not giving him a chance to say anything.

Kilo saw Correy slam the phone down and wondered what was going on. When Correy got up and started walking towards them, Mr. Lee walked off.

"What up with old school, why he walked?" asked Correy.

"I don't know. What up, you good? I seen you yelling on the phone," he said while Correy sat down.

"My nigga got a problem with something with what I had going on that end, but it's nothing."

"Oh yeah? What you got going on out there. It looks like you was getting a li'l cash when I use to see you."

Correy hesitated on answering his question because he really didn't know him. "Ya know I fuck around with a li'l work here and there so I'm still tryna make a few moves. What you got going on?"

"I got a squad out there, I'm sure you heard of 'em. We jack boys, but we only get niggas who are making big moves. It's six of us and we all about that, so niggas know not to fuck with us."

Correy's mind was racing a thousand miles per hour. He had heard about the squad but had never run across them. When he realized that Kilo could be a good asset, he decided to run a plan his way.

"Y'all niggas must be getting some paper the way you got Lexi turned up."

When Correy mentioned Lexi's name he tightened up because he hadn't heard from her since he'd been locked up.

"Yeah, I gets paper, but shit getting old, you feel me? I'm trying to do something different."

"What type of shit you talking 'bout?" Correy asked. He felt like this was his shot. He needed a squad and Kilo wanted to make a different move. Correy was already trying to put a million-dollar plan together.

"You know I ran across the couple of bricks while I was making a move, so I might do that, plus I got some cash put away for rainy days.

"Shit, I'm trying to take over some shit, but it's hard when you don't have too many niggas you could trust."

Kilo knew what he was getting at because they were getting at the same thing. He knew if he had a way to cop some more work and somebody who knew people to cop it, he and his squad could eat both ways.

"I could send some niggas ya homeboy's way so they could handle that issue he got going on."

"And what's that going run me, because I know it ain't free?" Correy asked with a suspicious look on his face.

"Nothing. Just a little something to show you what type of nigga you fucking wit, plus the new start of a business contract," he said while giving Correy dap.

"I'ma let you know how to get in contact with my nigga."

"I already know where to find him," Kilo said while walking off.

All Correy could do was laugh because he already knew what type of nigga he was dealing with.

*****

Illy, Slugga, Low-Key, and Babygurl had all met up at Low-Key's spot so they could make some cash. Even though they were two members short, it wasn't gonna stop them from eating. Illy was the last one to come so everybody was ready to get started.

"Alright, so what you got for us?" Illy asked.

"I been scoping out these niggas on the north side. They got two spots, but the thing is the one we want to hit got six niggas on guard 24 /7," explained Slugga.

"Shit, we've done bigger then that's so it don't mean shit," Low-Key boasted.

"Yeah, but just like we killas, these niggas is too. If we pull this off, we gonna have enough to get Kilo and Felony out and still be straight."

"So, what we waiting on?" Illy asked.

Slugga finished explaining what needed to be done and what role everybody would play. When everything was said and done they all started loading up. Babygurl had pulled Illy to the side before they started to leave the house.

"What's up, when you gone go see Kilo again?" Babygurl asked. You could tell she was missing Kilo by the look in her eyes and the way she was acting.

"I'm going tomorrow, but I'm taking Lexie up there." Illy said. "He wanna talk to me about some shit he wants me to handle."

"Tell him to call me," she said and then walked off.

Illy and Slugga rode with each other while Low-Key rode with Babygurl. Before Illy took off, he pulled up on the side of Low-Key then tossed him two walkie talkies.

"When we get in position, we use these," he said right before he pulled off.

Illy turned up his radio then sped off towards the highway. He was lost in his thoughts and surprised about how Slugga was running this job. He could tell he was Kilo's everyday nigga.

It took them twenty minutes to get to the Northside. Before he parked, he circled around the block a couple of times to check things out. When he realized this was a perfect lick his

138

adrenaline started to rush. He parked three houses down from the one they were about to hit then checked his rearview mirror to see if low-Key and Babygurl was behind them. When he didn't see them, he started looking around.

"Where the fuck they at?" he asked Slugga.

"Nigga, if you wasn't so excited about this lick and caught up in your thoughts, you would've heard me tell them to park around the corner on the other side of the house."

He shrugged him off then checked both of his 9mm. When he saw Slugga screw a silencer on his gun, he knew it was about to get ugly. He just hoped his squad came out on top. "Alright, I need y'all to go to the back and be ready just in case they try some slick shit. Remember, bust on anything you see moving," he explained through the walkie talkie. "Okay, let's move and get out of here."

They both jumped out then started walking towards the house. Once they saw them in their positions, they knew it was a go. Slugga was the first to climb the steps and then Illy. Illy knocked on the door and somebody answered before he could finish.

"Who is it?" a female voiced asked.

"What up, y'all got some killa or what?" Illy shot back.

He heard the door unlocking and when it opened, they saw a sexy-ass woman. "Y'all gon' stand there and stare or y'all gon' come in and cop something?" she asked with an attitude.

"As a matter of fact, we gonna cop everything you got in this bitch!" he said while grabbing her shirt then putting the banger to her head. He pushed her inside and then pulled out his other one as Slugga did the same.

"Please don't hurt me," she said in a whisper.

"Tell us what we want to know and I promise we won't," said Slugga. "Where the six niggas at that's on guard?"

139

"They in the back room counting money!"

"Okay, Low-Key, Babygurl, come through but be careful because they in the back," Slugga said through the walkie talkie.

Illy picked up the girl then started walking towards the back room. When they heard footsteps, they both turned to see where the noise was coming from. They saw that it was Low-Key and Babygurl and they both relaxed. All of them tiptoed to the room and listened to what was going on inside. Before Slugga could say something, Low-Key kicked the door open and Illy threw ol' girl inside. They walked inside with their guns drawn. They saw all of the money that was being counted on the bed and got excited. They were so caught up in the money that when they heard the front door open, they realize that it was only three niggas.

"If anybody move, smoke 'em," said Slugga as he crept of. Slugga was moving slowly because he didn't want to get surprised.

The noise came from the kitchen so he slid on the side of the wall and waited for whoever it was around the corner. As soon as he came around, he smashed his face with the butt of the gun. When he grabbed his nose, Slugga tried to kick him, but he was too big. The nigga was coming his way quickly, but Slugga already had his heat pointed at his head.

"Make another move and ya dead!" he said, out of breath.

As he finished his sentence, he heard a gunshot come from the back. He grabbed homeboy then headed back to the room. When he got back, one of the niggas was shot in the head.

"What the fuck he do?" he asked, regretting that Low-Key didn't have a silencer on his banger.

"He was reaching for his strap, so I offed the nigga." Low-Key said as he pointed to his gun.

"Y'all bitch-ass niggas won't get away with this!"

"Yeah we will, because, y'all won't live to tell," Illy said letting three shots off to his chest.

Babygurl did the other one on the bed, and Slugga popped the one he had on the head.

"Let her live. Pack this shit up so we can bounce," said Illy.

Ray Vinci

Chapter 22

Lexi, Lisa, and Lovey were sitting outside smoking a blunt and catching up on everything since a lot had been going on in the last month.

"So, what's up, girl, when is the baby due?" Lovey asked Lexie.

"In November. I got four more months. I can't wait!"

"Have you heard from Kilo? He's in there with Correy and he said Kilo got about another month to do," said Lovey.

"I'm going to go see him today. His brother and Slugga is coming to pick me and Lisa up in a li'l bit, but if he don't get his shit together, I'm done with him."

"Gurl, you ain't no good. You been trying to get with that nigga for years and now you just gon' dip on some bullshit," Lisa added while shaking her head.

Before Lexi could defend herself, Illy and Slugga were pulling up in front of Lovey's apartment. Lisa took off to the car and ran straight to the driver's side to give Slugga a kiss.

"That nigga must some good-ass dick the way he got a li'l sis acting," Lovey said, laughing and giving Lexi a high five.

"Girl, you crazy! I gotta go. I'll let you know what's up." She hugged Lovey jumped in the car.

She watched them until they drove off and then headed inside. As soon as she walked in, Quick was walking out of his room and justice boxers talking on the phone.

"Yeah, what time them niggas gon' come through so I can be ready?" Quick asked.

"About 1:00 p.m., so be ready," said Correy.

"Alright, let me jump in the shower."

"I'm out," Correy said and then hung up.

When he hung up, Lovey was staring at him.

"My bad."

"Naw you fine," she said, licking her lips.

Quick just looked back at her shook his head and walked to the shower.

When he was out of the sight, she went in the kitchen and started cooking breakfast. She had a lot on her mind. She was horny as hell. She had no dick in a long time, and this fine-ass nigga was staying in her house. She had made up her mind that she was gon' suck and fuck Quick today.

She heard the bathroom door open and snapped out of her thoughts. She was almost done when he walked back in. This time he had on basketball shorts and no shirt and Lovey found herself staring again.

"I think you starting to do that shit on purpose!" she said, tearing her eyes away from him.

"What you talking about?" he asked, confused.

"Alright, keep it up and you gon' find out," she said. "You hungry or what?"

"Hell yeah!"

Lovey fixed him a plate and he went to sit on the couch to eat. She made hers then went to the bedroom. When she was done, she changed into one of Correy's T shirts with just her panties underneath. She walked back in the kitchen and saw Quick staring at her.

"Girl, what you got going on? Go put some clothes on!" he said.

"You do it so I can, plus this is my house."

She put her plate up then went to sit next to Quick, all he could do was look her up and down. When she was walking to the kitchen, he saw how fat her ass was and the way it was shaking. He felt his dick getting hard just looking at her, so he tried to hide it.

"Why you hiding it? I done seen it before anyway," she said while facing him.

Quick found himself trying not to hide it and it looked like his dick was trying to bust through his shorts. Before he could tell her that it couldn't go down like that, she reached over and pulled his dick out of his shorts. She jacked him off slowly and when she saw his head fall back against the couch, she sped up. All of a sudden he felt the warmth of her mouth on his tip, so he adjusted so she could get to it more. Once she was comfortable, she went overtime on his dick. He tried to come back up because he was caught off-guard at how good the head was. When she finally came up for air, he was glad because he was about nut and he didn't want that. Before she could back down, he picked her up and carried her to the room.

As soon as he laid her down, she came out of her shirt and panties. He knew she was fine, but when she took off her clothes, he found out how fine she really was. He pushed her knees into her chest and then started sucking on her pussy.

"Oh! Ahhh!" she moaned. "Yes, oh God!"

Quick was eating her pussy so good that she cuffed the back of his head. He knew she was cumming because he could taste her juices all over his tongue. Lovey was shaking and squirming and so caught up in her nut that when Quick was entering her, she backed all the way up.

"Hold up, that's too much, so take it easy."

"All right, turn over."

When she turned over, she poked her ass in the air with her face in the mattress. He wasted no time and entered slow. She was so tight that he could only get the dick head in.

145

"Damn, girl, you tight as hell!" He said while slowly stroking.

She couldn't say anything because her face was in the pillow while her hands were clenching the sheets. He grabbed her waist and pushed in with one long stroke.

"Oh, fuck! Damn!" she yelled but wasn't able to finish what she was saying because he started fucking her. "Yes, baby, fuck my pussy! That shit feels good!"

"Damn, you got a fat ass," he said as he started making her ass shake. He had just gotten started getting into it when he saw his dick getting white, and he knew he was making her cum again.

"I…just came, daddy. Ooh, that dick is good!"

Lovey moved away then made him lay on his back so she could ride him. Once she straddled him, she took her time and bounced on half of it until she was sitting all the way down. She started riding him and couldn't believe she was taking so much. She rode him for fifteen minutes until he was finally about to cum.

"I'm about to cum." He felt hers coming too, but she jumped off.

"You turn now," she said and then slipped his dick in her mouth.

She put the whole thing in her mouth then popped up and down until she felt his dick starting to jump. She came up then started jacking him off and nut instantly started squirting, all over her face and titties. She was so surprised at how much he was cumming that she came just by seeing so much.

"Damn, boy, looks like you was backed up too," she said while squeezing the rest of his nut out.

"Girl, that shit was good, that's why it's so much."

"I know," she said, boasting.

146

He stood up and his dick was still hard.

"Damn, nigga, do you still want some more?" she said while looking at his dick. "I would, but my pussy and insides are on fire."

All he could do was laugh and put on his boxers. "So, what's gonna happen?" he asked.

"What do you mean? When I need a nut or you need one we holla, but we keep this to ourselves. Now let me get this shit off me."

Ray Vinci

Chapter 23

Quick was waiting on whoever Correy said he had coming to handle the problem he was having. He tried to ask him who and what they looked like, but he didn't want to say too much over the phone. He was really feeling fucked up about what him and Lovey had done so he didn't push it.

He was snapped out of his train of thoughts when he heard a knock on the door. When he went to open the door, he saw a familiar face and one he didn't recognize.

"What's up, gangsta? If you looking for Tre, he ain't here," said Quick.

"Nah, my brother told me about your problem, so we came to help you," Illy said.

"What's up, Illy, you know him?" Slugga asked him, confused.

"Yeah, I know him through my li'l homie Tre. So what's up with this problem?"

"Come in so we can handle this shit."

Illy and Slugga walked in the trap and then sat down at the table. Illy lit up a Newport and then checked the time. He saw it was 6:30 p.m. and he was ready to get this over with. Quick walked over to the table with a sack of doe-doe and some cigars.

"Alright, these niggas live around the corner. I don't know how many there is, but they pretty deep. I figured since they want me to quit grinding over here, they must be getting a lot of money, so they got a bounce!" he explained while hitting the blunt.

"If that's what you want, fuck it, let's make it happen," said Illy.

After they were done laying out the plan, they started getting ready. Illy checked his two 9mm's and pulled out two extra clips. Slugga pulled out his 40 cal. and some extra clips. Quick went to the back and then came back with a chocolate and two black and chrome 45's and gave one to Slugga.

"You gon' need more than that," he said. "Let's make a move."

Quick was the first one to leave out of the door Illy and Slugga followed.

It was night, so they felt comfortable. As they walked, they noticed that nobody was out. Illy and Slugga realized that they were going in blind with no layout of the apartment. When they made it to the apartment all the lights was on.

"Okay, when we get inside, nobody lives, so off everything," said Slugga.

Once Quick heard that, he stepped in front of the apartment and let loose his choppa. It was a full thirty seconds before he let up on the trigga. Illy and Slugga started for the door with Quick right behind them. Illy kicked open the door and when he did that, somebody started letting off shots at them from inside of the house. All three of them ducked out of the way of the bullets. Once the shots stopped Illy jumped up quick then dashed inside of the apartment. The first person he saw was a lady holding a gun, but he wasted no time pulling the trigga and dropping her where she stood.

Slugga and Quick back-doored him and came in shooting at the people that ran to the back room, but they missed. They all walked towards the back slowly, being cautious. Slugga kicked open the door and let loose as soon as he entered. Shots were fired from somewhere behind them, so they dove inside of the room.

"Get whoever that is shooting!" Illy said while yelling over the gunfire.

Right as he finished his sentence, someone came to the doorway and Slugga shot twice and dropped him. While Slugga was reloading, Illy and Quick were smoking everything that came through the door. Once everything seemed over, they all came out of the room, then searched the house to see if it was anybody left. They were content with everything they got. As they stepped outside, it seemed like everybody was staring at Quick while they walked to the trap. There was a sense of acknowledgement and respect.

"Damn, gangster, I didn't know you rode for yours like that, and I see you and no stranger at busting yo' guns neither," Quick said to Illy.

Illy lit up in Newport as they stood on the porch. For some reason after what they had just done, they felt at ease instead of being nervous.

"I got a feeling you might be that nigga after tonight," said Slugga while reaching for Illy's Newport.

"Shit, I just might. What I owe you?"

"Nothing. It was my big bro, yo' homie's, idea, so we good."

They both walked back to the car then jumped in

"Oh yeah, I'll be by in a couple of days to drop something off!" he yelled as he pulled off.

***

Lexi had just drove off of the impound lot with Kilo's truck when her phone rang. She was going to let it rain until she saw that it was Illy.

"Hello, what's up, bro?"

"What's up, sis, you handle that or what?"

"I just got his truck now. I'm on my way to the house right now. I'll call you when I'm ready."

She looked in her rearview mirror and spotted a car that looked familiar but couldn't place it. She decided to see if the car was following her and switched lanes. When she switched, the car switched too, so she turned a corner. As soon as she did that, she saw the car hit his lights and she instantly knew who it was. Now that she knew who it was, she got mad because she didn't have time for his bullshit. Lexi pulled over and Stronbone started walking towards the truck. When he got to the window, he had a smirk on his face as she rolled it down.

"What's up, little lady? Where have you been hiding? I need to ask you some questions about the shooting that went down."

"Look, I don't know shit and I don't know why they were shooting."

"Well, if you want to help Kilo and his homeboy, I suggest you cooperate, or they both will be in jail for a long time."

"If I'm not under arrest, I'm leaving, because all that bullshit-ass game you tryna run on me ain't gon' work," Lexi said, getting angry.

"Little pretty lady, I like your style, but when you never see Kilo again, it's gonna be your fault!" He walked off.

Lexi stared at the truck. She drove off with that conversation they just had on her mind. She didn't want to be going through this, but when she went to see Kilo, he told her that this was going to happen. She loved Kilo and promised him

152

that she was going to stay by his side no matter what happened. She wanted to call Illy and explain to him what just happened, but she didn't want him to get paranoid.

When she pulled up in front of the house, she had to calm down. She stepped out of the truck and walked to the door. It was weird because she hadn't stayed there since Kilo had been in jail. She hesitated before she put her key in the keyhole. When she went in, she went straight to the bedroom where Kilo told her to look and found what she was looking for. She checked both duffel bags. One had the five bricks that she was supposed to get to Illy, and the other was full of money that she was supposed to keep for herself. She grabbed both bags and headed towards the door. She felt nervous and knew why. As she walked out of the door and locked it, her phone rang loudly, causing her to jump.

"Hello?" she said through the phone while sounding nervous.

"Girl, what's wrong with you? Why you sounding like you all out of breath and shit?" Lisa asked.

"Nothing. I'm just tired."

"Well, I'm off work so come pick me up!"

"Okay, give me like fifteen minutes and I'll be there." She hung up called Illy.

"Yeah?" he answered.

"Say bro, I got 'em. Meet me at Chacho's because I got to pick up my sister from work."

"Okay. Be careful with all that shit, girl," Illy said and then hung up.

She got in the truck and pulled off slowly. She was so nervous riding with all that dope and money that she rode in silence and looked everywhere for the police. She stopped at a red light and thought she saw Detective Stronbone behind her, but she knew she was tripping. She jumped on the freeway then headed towards the Northeast.

It took her twelve minutes to get to Chacho's because she had the gas pedal to the floor. As soon as she pulled in the parking lot, she spotted her sister come out and walking towards the truck. Lisa jumped in and Lexi felt a little bit relaxed.

"Hey girl, let's leave because I don't even want to see the inside of a Chacho's no more today!"

"I'm waiting on Illy and Slugga."

"For what?" Lisa asked.

She explained everything she was doing and once she was done explaining, Illy pulled up on the side of her and blew the horn. She motioned for him to get inside of the truck and saw that Babygurl and Low-Key were with him too. Babygurl was staring at her but didn't look too long. Illy jumped in the back smelling like a pound of weed.

"Damn! Where the fire at?" Lisa asked.

"Your man got it. Go get some."

Lisa jumped out to go talk to Slugga and Lexi showed him the duffel bag with the five bricks. When everything was settled, she and Lisa left went straight to Lovey's house.

Chapter 24

Kilo had just got off the phone with Bianca when Correy had walked in the tank. He and Bianca had been spending a lot of time on the phone. She was even coming to visit him as his attorney, so they were getting close. You could tell that Correy had some good news by the smile that was on his face. He walked up to Kilo and gave him dap.

"What up, gangsta, where are you coming from?" Kilo asked.

"From court. I'm out this bitch either today or tomorrow. They gave me a year probation, but they might not ever see me," Correy said excitedly.

"That's what's up. I just got off the phone with my lawyer. She said that I go to court in three weeks and she gon' try to get me time served," Kilo said with excitement in his voice. "Lexi got them thangs to my little bro, so Quick should have 'em when you get out.

"Alright. When you get out I got you, so don't trip. I heard your squad put it down out there. Now we got the whole complex on lock."

"You know that's just a little something to show you that my squad is useful to you."

"Say, I'ma get up wit'cha. I gotta hit Lovey up so she can be ready."

Kilo and Correy went their separate ways. Kilo was walking towards the TV when he saw Mr. Lee staring at Correy as he got on the phone.

"What's up, Mr. Lee? What's up with you and Correy?

"It's something about him that just don't sit right with me. He been running around here talking about how he tryna find the nigga that killed his friend. Just watch yourself around here."

Kilo was thinking about what Mr. Lee was saying about Correy. Mr. Lee was always giving him advice, plus he liked him, so he made up his mind about bonding him out and looking out for him.

"I feel you. Good looking out. When you getting out of here, Mr. Lee?"

"Youngster, I got nowhere to go and my family don't give a shit about me."

"Well, I get out in a couple of weeks. I got you."

"At least somebody cares."

Kilo walked back downstairs and started watching TV. When he got in front of the TV, they were still talking about the murders that took place on the north side. He already knew that it was his squad because he had been telling Slugga about that spot. They were also talking about the shootout that happened in the Deerwood Apartments.

He knew his squad was out there making noise and he liked what he was seeing. Now all he had to do was make things happen with what he and Correy had going on. If Correy needed him to take over, that meant he really didn't have anybody on his team. A million thoughts were going through his head when Correy called him to the phone.

"Say, Lovey just told me to tell you that twelve been following Lexi around since you told her to get your truck and them thangs," Correy explained.

Kilo already knew that it was Detective Stronbone trying to find something on him, so he was following her.

"Tell her to tell Lexi she hasn't done nothing, so stay calm and don't talk."

Correy told Lovey what Kilo said and then started back with his conversation.

Kilo jumped on the phone to call Lexi.

***

Felony had just come from his attorney visit and she told him she could get him off on self-defense. Bianca was representing him on behalf of Kilo, so it was free of charge. Kilo kept his promise and made sure he had a good lawyer, plus he kept money on his books. Low-Key and Babygurl would come and visit him whenever they could, but he knew they were busy because he saw the news.

When he hit the corner and turned down the hallway, he spotted Ms. Jones. Ms. Jones was in her mid-twenties and looked hella pretty. She had a caramel complexion with short hair that went to her shoulders. She stood at 5'4" and weighed 125 pounds with an ass that would make your jaw drop.

"Felony, you know the procedure," she said with a smile.

He put his hands on the wall then spread his legs, ready to get pat searched. She started patting him down and when she got to his dick, she grabbed it and rubbed on it until it got hard.

"I knew you was packing something down there. I just had to see for myself," she said as she continued to rub on his dick.

"When you gonna let a nigga feel on you?" he asked.

"Whenever you get out. Shit, I just might let you feel something right now."

As soon as he turned around to face her, he saw little Joe hit the corner. Felony had been beefing with little Joe since middle school and was ready to throw hands. Ms. Jones saw them beefed up and interfered.

"Joe, get to your tank before I lock your ass up!"

Li'l Joe turned the other way and went on about his business.

"Look, go back to your tank. I'm gon' stop by and check on you. If you need anything, let me know. I work tomorrow."

He walked off as Ms. Jones blew him a kiss. He made a mental note that he was gonna get at Li'l Joe later on.

He couldn't believe what had just happened with Ms. Jones. He knew she liked him, but she was trying to get with him for real. He made it his first priority to pursue Ms. Jones and keep her on the team.

Chapter 25

Kilo stepped out of the county jail with one thing on his mind: getting up with Correy to start locking shit down. He was expecting Lexi to come pick him up, but he knew she was busy, so he asked somebody to use their phone so he could call a cab. When Kilo looked up, he saw a black BMW pull up and blow the horn. At first he looked around and everybody around him did the same thing. As he walked a little bit closer the window rolled down and that's when Bianca yelled his name.

"Kilo!"

All he could do was smile because he wasn't expecting her to be here to pick him up. Bianca got out of the car then ran and jumped on Kilo. She started kissing him as he grabbed her ass. He let her down and all she did was just smile at him.

"Damn, girl, what a nigga owe you for everything you've done?"

"Just give me some of that dick and we even," she said while tossing him the key then walking to the passenger side. "You know the way to my apartment, right?"

Kilo smiled and ran to get in the driver's side. He cranked up the car, turned up the music, and then drove off. He didn't know what to say, but he did know that he was gonna show her much love, just like she showed him.

"What's up, baby, what's on your mind?" she asked.

He was so into his thoughts that he didn't even see her staring at him.

"Naw, I was just thinking about how you was the main one holding me down when you didn't even have to. You showed me more love than my baby mama. Why?"

"Every man needs to have a woman to be by his side at all times, and I can be that if you let me."

He took a couple of seconds to look at her to see if she was for real. When he saw that she was being 100% real with him he looked back at the road.

"I love you, li'l mama, and yeah, you can be that one."

She leaned over to give him a kiss and she rubbed his face. "I love you too, daddy!"

She started unzipping his pants and pulled his dick out. In no time at all, she was taking him in the back of her throat. Kilo loved the way she didn't hesitate to please him, and before he knew it, he was about to cum.

"I'm about to bust!" he moaned.

She kept bobbing her head up and down on his dick as Kilo released his seed in her mouth. She made sure she swallowed every drop before she came back up.

"Damn, girl, where did all of that come from?" he asked while trying to catch his breath.

"It's more where that came from. Just wait until we get home," she said while smiling.

Kilo couldn't help but think about how this girl was the total package that any nigga could want.

He had just exited the highway to Stone Oak when she told him to stop by the weed house so she could buy something to smoke on. It took her all of two minutes to go in and come back out. He pulled the car up to the front of her apartment and they got out. He waited for her at the front of the car and when she got there, he picked her up and carried her to the front door. He put the key in the door without putting her down and as soon as he entered, he heard Valerie and Slugga's voices in the back. When he came in, Slugga and Bianca's cousin came up front.

"What up, gangsta? Long time no see," he said while giving Kilo dap.

"What's up, my nigga?"

Kilo was happy to see Slugga because he had a lot to chop it up about.

Slugga handed him the blunt he had lit and took a good hit.

"What's up, Val, how are you doing?" he asked.

"I'm good. You hungry or what?"

"Yeah, but I got some unfinished business," he said while looking at Bianca and licking his lips.

"Good, because she getting on my nerves. Kilo this, Kilo that," she said, teasing Bianca.

Kilo grabbed Bianca's hand and went to the back room.

***

Correy had just gotten all of Kilo's money together when he got a call from Quick telling him about some apartments down the street from their trap. He had been looking for shit to take over ever since he came home. As soon as he got off the phone with Quick, his phone rang again. He didn't even look to see who it was as he picked it up.

"What's up, Joe, talk to me, what do you need?" he said through the phone.

"What up, gangsta, this Kilo. I'm on my way to your trap right now."

"Yeah! Yeah! I'm at the trap right now and I got your bread ready," Correy said with excitement. "I need to holler at you too."

"Alright, give me about ten minutes because I got to drop Lexi off with Lovey."

"Bet!" he said and then hung up.

Correy was happy that Kilo got in touch with him. That meant they could get started with their little plan they had. He thought that maybe Kilo could help him find the female and whoever it was that killed Rico. By the time Quick came, Correy was in deep thought.

"Damn, nigga, you didn't hear me come in?" he asked Correy, snapping him out of his thoughts.

"No. That nigga Kilo should be here in a few minutes so we can handle that shit in them apartments."

"Alright."

Right when he said that he heard loud music outside of his door. He and Quick jumped up with their straps in their hands. Ever since that shit went down with Quick and them niggas, police and niggas were around being curious. When they opened the door they saw Kilo, Illy, and Slugga.

"What's up with it, Joe, you alright?" he asked while giving Kilo dap.

"Yeah, just glad to be out of that bullshit-ass county jail."

They finished giving each other dap, then headed inside. As soon as they got in the apartment, Kilo didn't hesitate to get down to business.

"So, what you got for me?" asked Kilo.

As far as Kilo was concerned, this was only about money so he got straight to it.

"Here you go," Correy said while giving him a duffel bag full of money. "That's $125,000 for the bricks you sold me."

"That's what I'm talking about. What's up with taking over the city?"

"Speaking of that, I got some apartments on the list, but first let's get out and have some fun," Correy said.

"Alright, that's a bet. Let's meet up at Taboo's tonight," Kilo said.

Alright, I'll catch you later."

Kilo, Illy, and Slugga jumped in the truck and smashed off. Correy wanted to meet up with his whole crew to get a feel for them and see what type of nigga Kilo really was.

"What's up? I got some hoes in them apartments I was telling you about. Let's go check them out," said Quick.

"Cool, let me jump in the shower."

***

Correy had pulled up in the Artesians off of Benz-Engleman and I-35. It was jumping with the money. Quick told him where to go and spotted niggas sitting outside.

"That's the spot right there, plus your homeboys got another spot around the corner. The bitches we 'bout to get up with is related to them niggas," Quick explained.

"Oh yeah! So, you've been putting in some work, huh? These hoes bet' not be ugly. You know how you is," he said, laughing.

"Fuck you."

Correy had pulled up in front of the apartment Quick was talking about and couldn't wait to see who he was talking about. He got on the phone to let ole girl know that they were outside. When Correy saw how she looked, all he could do was smile. She was 5'1" with a long black ponytail. She was chocolate with almond eyes and weighed 120 pounds. Quick

Ray Vinci

jumped out and wasted no time showing her some love. He could tell li'l mama had a body even though she had on her pajamas. He saw Quick wave for him to get out of the truck, and when he got out, he felt somebody staring at him. He looked down the way and saw the same niggas that they were scoping out when they came in.

"Y'all make yourself at home. My friend in the back getting dressed. I'll be back," Nikki said.

"Alright, don't be too long." Quick pulled out a zone of weed. He saw a smile on her face and knew she was game.

"So, what's up, what you think?"

"We need to get these ASAP 'cause it look like they flooded with cash," said Correy.

They stopped talking when they heard the back-room door open. When Correy saw who came out, his eyes got big and his jaw dropped. Li'l mama was half-black, half-Asian with a light skin complexion. She was 5'9", 150 pounds of pure ass and titties. Her ass was so fat that he could see it from the front.

"Damn, little mama, what's yo' name?" Correy said while grabbing her hands. "Come sit next to a nigga."

"My name is Japan," she said while smiling, then she sat next to him.

He lit up a blunt and then passed it to her just as quick as he lit it. Nikki came from the back room talking on the phone and when she saw everybody looking at her, she hung up.

"My cousin on his way to drop off some weed, so just chill."

Right when she finished her sentence, there was a knock on the door. At the same time, Correy and Quick felt for their straps. When Nikki opened the door, two niggas came in and eyed them before handling business. They walked to the back and they both looked at each other. It didn't take long for them to come back up front

"What up, homie, where are y'all from?"

"The east side – northeast side," Quick said.

"Chicago."

"It looks like you're eating out here."

"Just a little bit; not much."

"Alrighty, holler if y'all need something."

Correy was heated at how they came at him and at that point, he decided to get at them quicker than planned.

Ray Vinci

Chapter 26

Kilo, Slugga, and Babygurl pulled up in front of Taboo's with
Illy and Low-Key right behind them. It took them a good fifteen minutes to get in the club and lock down VIP. Once they
began drinking, Illy was the first one to spot Correy, Quick,
Tre, and Keisha.

"Say, big bro, there go yo' boy and his team!" he said over
the music.

When Kilo saw Correy and his team, he stood up and
waved him over. Kilo was dressed normal but was still fresh
from head to toe. He had on some all-black Retro 12's to
match his Brooklyn Nets snapback. His gray 501's and his
plain white T-shirt made his platinum chain and watch stand
out.

Once Correy and his team made it to VIP, they greeted
each other, but Correy spotted a face he knew too well. He had
to make sure she was the same girl that he saw with Rico.
When he realized that it was her, he instantly got mad. He had
to know for sure that it was her that did it, so he decided not
to do anything just yet. Kilo saw how Correy was looking at
Babygurl and said something.

"What's up, gangster, you alright?" Kilo asked.

"Yeah, who is shorty?" he said, nodding at Babygurl.

"Naw, gangsta, that's off limits right there."

Correy started laughing because Babygurl was bad as hell
and he couldn't help but notice.

Everybody sat down as they poured drinks and got to
know each other. They all talked about the roles that each one
would play in the new deal they had going on. The whole time

they were discussing business, Correy kept shooting glances at Babygurl. Babygurl was trying to figure out where she saw Correy at before but couldn't place his face.

"Kilo, I'm going to the bar to get something else to drink." She got up and headed towards the bar.

"I'm going too," Keisha said as she was trying to catch up with Babygurl. When she caught up with her, she was already sipping on her drink.

"What's up, girl, you alright?" asked Keisha as she sat next to her.

Babygurl looked at her to see what she was getting at. "Shit, I just got tired of sitting around all them niggas."

"I feel you." She reached for her drink.

Babygurl and Keisha sat at the bar and talked while they sipped their drinks. You could tell that they were both tipsy by the way their words slurred.

Keisha stood up and staggered back a little bit. "Damn, girl, I gotta go to the restroom. I'll be back."

"I got to go too."

As they made their way towards the restroom, they were turning heads because they were two of the baddest bitches in the club. Keisha thought she heard one of the females talking shit, but she had to use the bathroom bad as hell so she let it pass.

By the time she and Babygurl came out, she heard the same bitch talking shit, but this time she was around some niggas.

"Them hoes think they the shit," ole girl said.

Keisha's comeback was so quick that it caught ole girl by surprise.

"Bitch, you must think with this shit because you're doing a lot of hating!" Keisha shot back.

She didn't like what she heard because she stepped to Keisha like she was ready to scrabble. Keisha didn't waste time slapping her in the mouth. It caught Babygurl by surprise because she didn't know Keisha was about to do it. When she saw her slap her, she began liking her even more. Once she hit her back and stumbled Keisha, Babygurl jumped in with three punches of her own. Keisha got her balance and got back in to help Babygurl.

Babygurl already had her hair wrapped around her hand and was punching her anywhere her fist landed. Keisha was already pushing her down to the ground so they could stomp her out. When they finally got her down, they landed their feet all over her head. One of the niggas she was with grabbed Keisha then swung her to the ground and did the same to Babygurl.

"Bitch-ass nigga! You better watch who the fuck you putting your hands on!" yelled Keisha.

"Bitch, move around before I slap your ass!" he yelled back.

"You gon' be sorry for putting your hands on me!" Babygurl said as she grabbed Keisha and walked off.

When they made it back to VIP, everybody was standing up looking at the crowd they had just come from. Once Kilo saw that they were looking like they just got into a fight, he started looking at her face.

"What happened to you?" he asked Babygurl.

"We just stomped one of them hating-ass bitches out!" she responded. "And one of them niggas put their hands on us!"

That caught all of their attention as they all look towards the back of the club.

"Where they at?" Quick asked, ready to go to war with whoever.

169

"No, let's go outside and wait. Somebody gotta die for touching mines," said Kilo.

Both squads made their way to their rides and strapped up. Kilo tucked his 40 cal. behind his back while Correy kept his in his hand and sat on the hood of his truck.

"Y'all let me know who them niggas is and it's a go," said Kilo.

Five minutes after they strapped up, they saw a group of niggas and females coming out of the club being loud. Kilo knew it was them because one of the females was beat up.

Before Kilo or anybody could say something, Babygurl started letting off shots towards the group. Illy was right behind her with both his 9mm, trying to hit anything in his path. Before they knew it, everybody was walking up hitting everything that was moving. Once they felt like everybody was gone, they started running back to their rides, except Babygurl and Keisha. They had been looking for the nigga who pulled them off of ole girl. As soon as Babygurl spotted him hiding behind one of the cars, she ran up on him.

"Who are you going to slap now, bitch-ass nigga?"

She released her whole clip in his body as Keisha watched in surprise. Both of them ran back to their squad when they heard the police sirens.

***

Lexi, Lovey, and Lisa were sitting on Lovey's sofa while Lovey was telling them how she and Quick were still messing around.

"Bitch, you trippin'. Correy gonna kill you and that nigga if he finds out," Lexi said.

"That's the point. He ain't gonna find out, and I ain't gonna stop fucking the nigga either," she responded.

"Let me find out you feelin' him in more ways than one?" Lisa asked.

When Lovey didn't respond back and put her head down, they already knew her answer. She didn't know that she was gonna catch feelings for Quick, so it caught her by surprise. To her it was gonna only be a quick fuck because Correy was in jail, but now that he was out, she still wanted to fuck with him. She started wondering if Quick felt the same way.

She was snapped out of her thoughts when she heard Lexi telling her to get the door. She opened it and Correy, Quick, Kilo, and Slugga walked in. Lexi was happy to see Kilo because she was having pains and she was tired. Everybody said their goodbyes and then headed out the door.

Before Kilo got in the truck, Correy yelled and told him, "Don't forget about tomorrow!"

Kilo nodded and pulled off.

Slugga and Lisa were in the back when they heard Lexi groan in pain.

"Half-breed, you alright?"

"No, I think this baby tryna come!" she said while grabbing her belly.

Kilo didn't ask questions and smashed off towards Baptise Hospital. It took him no time getting there. He got Lexi out of the front with Lisa's help and then walked her inside the hospital. Once they let the nurse know that she was having the baby, the nurse took over.

Lisa and Slugga stayed in the waiting room while Kilo went to the back. It was two hours before Kilo came back out to announce that he had a baby girl. When he looked around, his whole squad was waiting on them, including Lovey.

171

"Can we go see my sister now?" asked Lisa.

"Yeah."

Lisa and Lovey took off towards the back to see Lexi and the baby.

"Thank you for coming."

"Congratulations, big bro!" Illy said while hugging him.

The whole squad gave him daps and hugs, including Baby-gurl. They all walked outside so they could smoke, but when they walked outside, Detective Stronbone was sitting on the hood of his car with his partner.

"Well, well, if it ain't Mr. Kilo. What do you got going on here? That little pretty lady of yours having your baby?" said Stronbone.

"Mind your fucking business, pig!" Kilo said while lighting a cigarette.

"You right, might as well get down to why I'm here. Some shit went down at Taboo's and it's got you and your squad's name all over it," he said while pointing at all of them.

"Don't know what you're talking about, Detective," said Kilo.

"Well, you know somebody going to talk and I hope they say y'all black asses was at the scene," he said, getting in his car. "I'm watching y'all, and congrats."

When Detectives Stronbone left, everybody stayed quiet. Kilo was mad and couldn't believe this shit. Everybody walked back inside with a lot on their minds.

Chapter 27

Kilo had just dropped Lexi and the baby off at the house then took right back off. He told Lexi that he needed time to think. He decided to hit Bianca up and kick it with her until it was time to handle business. He turned up the Future he had playing then sped down the highway. He had finally made it to Stone Oak when his phone rang.

"Talk to me," he said through the phone.

"What's up, when you wanna come by and kick it?"

Kilo knew who it was because she tried to disguise her voice but couldn't because her white voice overpowered it. He decided to play with her since she felt like playing.

"I might come through tomorrow or the next day. I'm busy right now," he said while smiling and turning into her apartment.

"Well, I'll see you tomorrow," she said and then hung up.

He couldn't do anything but laugh because he could tell she was mad. He pulled up in front of her apartment, rolled down all his windows, turned up the music, then got out to stand in front of his truck. The door opened and Bianca stood there smiling at him. She walked to him and gave him a hug and kiss him.

"You play too much. Why you lie to me?"

"You were playing, so I decided to play with you," he said while slapping her on the ass. She still had on her PJ's so that ass was looking even fatter. He noticed that she was gaining weight but was getting thicker at the same time.

"Girl, that ass getting fatter and fatter every time I see it," he said while grabbing it.

"Well, you keep fucking me the way you doing it's gon' keep getting fatter."

As he grabbed her then walked in the house, he smelled something cooking and his stomach started growling.

"You hungry, baby?"

"Hell yeah!" He sat down on the couch. "Where is Val?"

"She's at work today."

She went in the kitchen then came back with his plate. She had made some chicken Alfredo with some butter garlic bread and some Kool-Aid. Kilo ate as he explained to her how Lexi had the baby yesterday.

"So, you happy, right?" she asked because of the look on his face.

"Yeah, but things are starting to change. She act like she didn't want to hold me down when I was gone."

Bianca knew what he meant because they had talked about it before while he was locked up. She wanted Kilo to be with her, but she also wanted him to handle his business. She understood that he was in the streets and she hoped she could talk him into leaving them.

"You could move in with me, or we could get a bigger house."

He was caught off-guard by what she said and looked at her to see if she was serious. That didn't sound like a bad idea because he needed a spot where nobody knew where he was. He was also thinking about Lexi and how he loved her and couldn't just leave her. He had already decided to get Lexi out of that house and put her and the baby in a good place to live.

"Let me think about it. I'm tired right now," he said as he finished his plate.

She put his plate up and when she came back, she and Kilo went to the bedroom and fell asleep.

***

Kilo woke up to the sound of his phone playing French Montana so he couldn't ignore it.

"Hello."

"What up, gangsta, where are you at? It's about time," Illy said.

When Kilo looked at the time, he jumped up. It was 6:00 p.m. and he had to get ready for the job they had. In the process of him getting ready, Bianca got up. She just stared at him while he got dressed.

"I got to handle some business."

"Okay, call me when you get a chance."

He got in his truck then turned up his Li'l Boosie to get in his zone. He must have really been in a zone because he almost passed up his exit. By the time he got to Correy's trap house, his whole squad was standing outside waiting on him. As he stepped out of his truck, Correy, Quick, and Tre came out of the apartment.

"What up? Let's get to it, I got Lexi waiting on me."

"Let's go inside and go over everything," said Correy.

Everybody went inside and Correy got to explaining everything while Quick added his two cents in. When they were done, Kilo let him know if he wanted to get this done that he do things his way. He intended to let him know he wasn't the boss of shit. He already didn't like the way he was trying to run shit.

When everything was said and done, they all made their way to Benz-Engleman. Once they got there, they saw what Correy was talking about. Kilo signaled everybody to pull over by the pool.

"Illy and Slugga, y'all go in next to me. Low-key and Babygurl, you're right behind Correy, Quick, and Tre, make sure nobody comes in from other trap," Kilo said. "Whatever is, moving blast 'em."

They all jumped out of their rides then started checking their traps while Correy pulled Kilo to the side.

"What up, Joe? When you finish with this, we're gonna need some help running this shit. If you're tryna flip that bread, we can go in or something," he said to Kilo.

"Yeah, we can do that, but let's get these niggas first, then we can chop it up," Kilo said while giving him dap.

Everybody started walking towards the trap and as soon as they hit the corner, all eyes were on them. One of the niggas sitting in front of the trap sat up and said something.

"Yeah, straight or wet."

Kilo just pulled out his strap and hit ole boy in the chest twice and once in the head. Before his crew even knew what was going on, Illy and Slugga were already shooting everything out there. Kilo heard shots from the back and knew niggas were coming from the other trap. All Correy saw was niggas and sparks coming his way, but he still managed to keep his eyes on Babygurl. He saw how she was holding her own by dropping everything with no more than three shots. He couldn't help but think how she was beautiful and a gangsta: a deadly combo. He was caught off-guard by being knocked to the ground by one of the niggas from the trap. When he looked up and saw the nigga he was talking to the other day, he knew he was dead. Before homie could shoot, his head exploded and his body fell to the ground. Babygurl handed him his gun and went back to work.

Kilo was re-loading his gun and looking for Babygurl at the same time. There were a lot of niggas and Kilo realized that he came in this shit blind and got mad at the thought. When he came from behind the car, he spotted Babygurl and everybody from his crew. He got alongside of her and walked inside of the track. Illy saw them go inside so he made sure they watched the door. He knew they had it under control so he yelled to Low-Key and Slugga.

"Go check the other spot and get what you can!"

Quick watched any movement going towards the door and shot at it. When he saw Tre and Correy dropping what seemed like the last of them, his heart started beating slower. By the time they got back together, nobody was outside. Correy was looking at Babygurl because she saved his life, but he still had to smoke her if it was her. They got in their rides then headed back to Correy's spot.

***

They were all sitting in the living room smoking weed when Correy thanked Babygurl.

"Say...thank you for what you did."

"It was nothing." She went to sit next to Kilo because she didn't feel right around Correy.

Kilo tried to give Corey and his boys half of what they got, but he denied it because he knew his squad had to eat. If everything kept going like this, they all would eat and he would make sure of it.

"What's up with what we talked about?" Correy asked Kilo while passing him a blunt.

"Yeah, we can do something."

"I want to put Quick out there with two of your boys, and I need half that money I gave you so we can cop something big, so by tomorrow we can have at the Artesians setting up shop."

Kilo had split one half of the money with his squad and had planned on copping something with the other half anyway. He decided to put Illy and Low-Key with Quick so they could make some money.

"Alright, hit me up later on so you can get the money. I'm gon' put Illy and Low-Key with Quick," he said while shaking Correy's hand to seal the deal.

Chapter 28

Kilo was up playing with his daughter Heaven when Lexi came out of the shower. She gave him a kiss and he realized how much he loved her. He couldn't leave them.

Today Felony was coming home and Kilo needed him, plus he was bonding out Mr. Lee. Once Kilo got dressed, they jumped in the truck and drove off. He was deep in his thoughts when Lexi snapped him out of them.

"What's up, baby, what's on your mind? Talk to me," she said while grabbing his hand.

"Just thinking about how I want you to find another place to live, so you and my baby can be safe. I want you to find a house so nobody knows where we stay, and not no bullshit-ass house. A good one."

"Okay, I'm glad, because I don't want my baby around no bullshit."

They talked about everything like they used to and Kilo liked that. Before they jumped on I-10 he stopped at Fernando's Bail Bonds and bailed Mr. Lee out. He got in and drove the back streets all the way to the county jail. Kilo thought about how his squad was making more money than they had ever seen, but he still scoping out licks just in case it went wrong. Babygurl was telling him how she knew Correy from somewhere, plus Mr. Lee told him that he was no good.

When they pulled up to the jailhouse people were standing outside, but none of them was Felony or Mr. Lee. Kilo stepped out of the truck to smoke a Newport. When he walked around to let Lexi hit it he saw Felony. Once Lexi spotted him she got out.

"What up, gangsta? You looking like new money. I can tell y'all been doing it big!" said Felony while giving him dap.

"You know we got some new shit going on. I'm glad you out because we need you, you ready to get this paper what?"

"Fa sho'. What's up, Lexi? Appreciate you coming to see me, I know you got some weed," he said while hugging her.

"Yeah, I ain't forgot about you," she said, laughing.

"Damn, where yo' stomach go?"

"I had the baby last week."

She saw Kilo walking towards someone that she didn't recognize, which made Felony turn around. Once she shook his hand she felt at ease. Kilo and Mr. Lee walked back to the whip and Kilo introduced them.

"Let's move from here. Ain't even trying to look at this place no more," Felony said as they jumped in the truck and smashed off.

"Looks like you're doing good for ya'self, youngster."

"Yeah, I'm good. I gotta to talk to you about some shit later."

"Let me get a smoke."

He handed him a Newport and picked up his phone at the same time. He dialed Slugga's number then waited. When Slugga pick up, he motioned for Felony to be quiet.

"What up, nigga, where you at?" asked Kilo

"At the mall with Lisa, what's up?"

"I got a surprise for y'all. Get the squad together. Meet me at the spot."

"Cool," Slugga said and then hung up.

Kilo caught Felony up on what was going on and filled Mr. Lee in on what he didn't know. Lexi had a little Sweet and passed it to Kilo. He hit it a few times then passed it to the back. Mr. Lee didn't smoke so Felony grabbed it then hit it as hard as he could and started choking. They all started laughing because he didn't know it was doe-doe.

It didn't take Kilo much time to get to his place. Lexi got out, grabbed Heaven, and walked in the house with everybody right behind her. Felony and Mr. Lee sat on the couch but before they could get comfortable Kilo told Mr. Lee to follow him to the back so they could talk.

"What up, youngsta, talk to me."

"Look, I know you don't have nowhere to go, so you can have this room right here for now. We can go shopping for some shit later. Here go a li'l cash to have in your pocket until I can get you set up somewhere."

Mr. Lee counted it out to $500 and then stuffed it in his pockets. "I appreciate everything you doing for me, youngsta," he said and then hugged Kilo.

"It's nothing. Just stick by my side and I got you."

They walked back up front and as soon as they made it to the living room, the door opened.

"Knock, knock!" Lisa said and walked to the room where Lexi was. Kilo heard his squad outside and he, Felony, and Mr. Lee walked outside. Once they saw Felony they started yelling and giving him dap.

"We got to celebrate," said Illy.

"Hell yeah," Felony shot back as everybody started dropping money on him.

"Say y'all, this my old school Mr. Lee. He gon' be rocking with us from now on," Kilo said.

They all gave him dap and introduced themselves and Babygurl gave him a hug. He explained that he had just got out of jail and they dropped a couple $100 on him too.

"I got another surprise for y'all tonight before we go out, meet us back here."

"I got to get something to wear," said Felony.

"Don't worry, let's go to the mall. I got you," said Low-Key.

"I need something too," said Mr. Lee

"We are on our way right now," said Kilo.

Everybody went their way as Lexi came out with the baby and got in the truck. Kilo turned up the Da Baby then smashed off. It took him 30 minutes to get to Ingram Mall. When they got inside of the mall Mr. Lee went his way and they walked into the jewelry store.

"What's up, Kilo? We just got your product in," the store owner said in an Arabian accent.

"What up, Omar? This Lexi and Heaven. Let me see what you got for me."

He went to the back and came back with one big box and two small boxes. He handed him the two small boxes first and the first one he opened had a necklace with the letter H on it. When Lexi saw it, she got happy.

"Aww, baby, it's so pretty, she's gonna love it!" she said while putting it around Heaven's neck. She was so caught up that she didn't see him open the other box. When she saw the 24k necklace with diamonds encrusted on it and the matching earrings, she started crying. He put the necklace on her and told her he love her while she put the earrings on.

"Thank you, baby."

"You're welcome. Anything for my queen."

By the time he started opening the big box, Mr. Lee had walked in with two bags and two boxes of shoes. He opened the box and pulled out one of the chains that was in it. The chain was 14k with diamonds all around it and said "The Squad" with diamonds around it also. Kilo was happy and all he could do was smile.

"That's what I'm talking about right there," Mr. Lee said.

"Hell yeah!" he said and then put the chain around his neck. Since everything was paid for, he copped some earrings and a bracelet to match. After he paid for them, he headed towards his truck and left.

Ray Vinci

Chapter 29

Kilo had just finished getting dressed when Lexi came in the room with the Sweet lit. He had on some True Legend jeans, a black color polo shirt, and black on black Air Force ones, with a black and white Chicago Bulls snapback, plus the jewelry he bought at the mall.

"Let me take a picture of you, baby," Lexi said while grabbing her phone. He posed so she could snap then passed the blunt back to her.

"Tomorrow, I want you to start looking for us another place to stay," Kilo said while hugging her.

"Me and my sister Lisa's going."

Before he could say anything back there was a knock at the door. "Come in!" he yelled.

Mr. Lee came in dressed in Polo from head to toe.

"Damn, Mr. Lee, you look like you're twenty-five years old!" said Kilo.

"I'm still young. Don't judge a book by its cover."

"You look nice, Mr. Lee," said Lexi then walked out of the door.

"Ya squad is out there, youngsta."

"Alright, tell 'em I'm coming."

Mr. Lee walked out and left Kilo alone. He lit a cigarette and thought about how far they had come. Now every one of his squad members had their own spot, and their names were known and fear. He also had soldiers in each apartment they had in case some shit went down. Correy even had a little team that was eating. Once he finished his Newport, he grab the jewelry box then walk to the living room where his squad was.

185

"Hey, Kilo," Babygurl said.

Babygurl and Lexi still didn't like each other, but they had no choice but to tolerate each other.

"What up, Babygurl?" he shot back.

"Damn, nigga, when you get that fat-ass chain?" Illy asked in amazement.

"Earlier today. Listen, y'all been loyal to a nigga since day one. I told y'all we gon' make it to the top and we halfway there so I just wanted to show y'all appreciate y'all." He pulled out the black box and showed six chains.

The whole squad started grabbing the chains and putting them on. There was one left, so Kilo grabbed it.

"Mr. Lee, I know you only been with the squad for a little bit, but you still a part of us." He handed him the chain.

"Alrighty, youngsta."

"Now, let's go shut the club down."

***

Since everybody had their own spot, Correy gave Keisha and Babygurl Deerwood. He still kept a lot of his own work and money there that they didn't know about. He had walked in the trap thinking nobody was there. He walked straight to the room where he kept a lock on the door. He walked inside of the closet and pulled out three bricks and some money. Before he came out of the closet he heard a noise come from the kitchen. He instantly pulled out his strap and walked out of the room.

As he entered the kitchen with the gun pointed in front of him, Keisha turned around and screamed.

"Damn, girl, I almost shot yo' ass!" He put his gun away. "I didn't think no one was here."

"I was asleep. I didn't hear you come in. It was so much money last night I just stayed."

All she had on was a shirt and he could tell she didn't have nothing on under it by the way her titties moved. She saw him looking but didn't pay him mind. When she reached in the cabinet to get a cup her shirt raised up and Correy saw her ass hanging out of the bottom of the shirt.

"You want something to drink?" she asked, snapping him from her ass.

"Naw, I'm just grabbing some shit. I'm about to bounce." He walked off all she could do was laugh as he left. He was in the room putting the money and the bricks in the bag when Keisha walked in.

"What's up, boy, why did you walk away from the kitchen?"

"Girl, you trippin'. What are you talking about?"

"You know you like what you see so stop tripping." She walked up on him and kissed him then grabbed his dick. "I've been trying to fuck you since day one but you didn't notice."

Correy's dick was getting hard as she pulled it out of his pants. She began jacking it in her mouth as his pants and boxers fell to the floor. He sat down and then lay back on the bed so she could go to work. She wasted no time putting his dick in her mouth. With skill, she soaked his wood with saliva.

"Ah, damn, girl!" he groaned as he grab the back of her head. All you heard was gargling, gagging, and spitting as she worked her magic.

"I'm finna cum!"

To his surprise, she kept sucking his dick, swallowing every drop she could. She got up, wiped her mouth, and went back to the kitchen. He was fucked up about that because he wanted to fuck. He stayed in the room a little while to gain his

composure and smoked a Newport. Once he was done smoking, he walked to the kitchen where she was. He dropped a
duffel bag by the table and walked straight to her. He turned
around and bent her over the counter, lifted her skirt, and entered her. This caught her by surprise, so she yelled.

"Oh shit!"

He grabbed her hair and started pulling it as he ran his dick
as far as it could go.

"Ohhh! Yes, fuck this pussy!" she moaned. "You got a fat
dick, boy!"

She was wiggling and squirming trying to get away, but
he had her locked.

"I'm cu...cum...cumming!" she moaned.

"You like this shit, don't you?"

"Hell, yeah I do!"

He backed up and pulled his dick out so he could get a
look at her ass. Her ass was super fat, but her pussy was swol-
len from all the pounding so it stuck out. She turned around
and he picked her up. When he put his dick back in it felt
tighter than before. She was so turned on by how Correy was
handling her that she started bouncing on his dick.

"Damn, it's too much, fuck!" she said as she kept bouncing.

"Take this dick!"

"I am cumming again."

As she said that, he started sucking her titties and she released all of her juices over his dick he kept fucking because
he was about to come. He made her get off and get on her
knees and she started jacking him off until he came. He nutted
all over her face and when she was done she stood up.

"Thank you, I needed that." She walked off.

She was red in the face so he knew he fucked her good. He wiped his dick off, grabbed the bag, then left. He didn't want to be around her when she came out.

He jumped in his ride and pulled off and thought about how far he made it. He and Kilo owned half of San Antonio and it had only been a few months. Whoever was selling dope was getting it from them and whoever wasn't was getting popped off.

He decided to run it by Kilo to help him find out who killed his homeboy. The whole time Correy was in his thoughts he didn't see Detective Stronbone following him.

Ray Vinci

Chapter 30

Everybody met up at Kilo's spots to collect the work they needed. Kilo had made this their get together spot since Lexi had found them a spot on the northside. Bianca had also found him a place of Ingram Road. So, nobody knew where he would be. Kilo, Illy, Felony, Slugga, Low-Key, Babygurl, Mr. Lee, and a few people Kilo had hustling in his spot were there. Correy, Quick, Tre, Philly, Tidy, Keisha, and some of the people Correy put on were also there. There were blunts and Ciroc bottles everywhere so everybody was feeling good. Babygurl and Keisha had gotten real close since that incident at the club and since neither one of them had been tight with anybody before, it made them a deadly combination. Kilo saw Correy wave him over, so he walked to him.

"What up, gangsta? Talk to me."

"Let's talk on the porch," said Correy

When they got outside he looked at every car out there and he realized that they were moving kind of fast.

"Look out, Joe. About a year ago some niggas killed my homeboy, who was like my brother. They hit him after we made a move so they got him for everything. I've been trying to find out who smoked him, but I don't know who did it. All I know is that he was with a Mexican bitch last time I saw him."

Kilo could tell he was getting mad as he spoke, so he hit the Sweet then passed it to him. Out of nowhere it finally hit him as the memory of Rico came to his mind, and his first thought was Babygurl. He didn't want to look suspicious to Correy, so he hit him back

"You know it's whatever. I know some niggas, so let me find something out and we gon' ride for sure, my nigga," said Kilo with a serious face. "As a matter of fact, let me talk to my crew and see what's up."

"I appreciate that."

He gave Kilo dap as he stepped back inside. As Kilo was going in, Quick was coming out.

"What up, my nigga, you alright?" Quick asked, reaching for the blunt he was hitting.

"Yeah, I'm good, what's on your mind?"

"Remember when I told you that I knew that nigga Felony from somewhere?"

"Yeah, what about him?" Correy said, looking at him suspiciously.

"He was the nigga scoping us out when we first got the trap."

"You sho' right."

Correy started wondering what type of shit Kilo had going on. First, he knew for sure that Babygurl was the bitch that was with Rico, now Felony was the nigga scoping them out, plus he remembered seeing Felony in jail. He ran everything down from Babygurl, Rico, and Felony. He told Quick to keep an eye out on everybody in Kilo's squad. Correy was gon' get down to the bottom of this even if it killed him. He hoped he didn't have anything to do with it Kilo because he didn't want no beef with him in any kind of way. He decided to let it go for now and see what Kilo came up with but was going to watch Babygurl and Felony case.

***

192

Babygurl was dressed in some blue jean shorts that showed off her thighs, a pink muscle shirt, and some pink and white high-top Chuck Taylors. Keisha wore some black tights that showed her ass, a white muscle shirt, and some white-on-white Air Max 90's. They were walking through Deerwood making sales and turning heads. They were the baddest bitches in the apartment complex. There were sales coming left and right so they posted up by the pool.

"It's jumping out here. We should have brought some weed with us," Keisha said.

"Hell yeah!"

As if on point, a nigga got out of the pool and walked up to them.

"I know where y'all can get some right now."

"Where at? Take me and I'll break you off a Sweet or two," said Babygurl.

"Cool, follow me," he said, getting dressed.

They followed him around the corner to a spot they weren't familiar with. Off the top she started regretting leaving her strap. He knocked two times and a nigga answered that was cute as hell, so she relaxed.

"Damn, Jr., where you find these at?" he asked, eyeing both of them up and down.

"They want some weed, Prince."

"Come in."

When they walked in there was another nigga sitting at the table bagging what looked like some fire-ass doe-doe.

"What y'all want?" asked Prince.

"An ounce of what he bagging up." Keisha said.

"Damn, y'all ballin' like that?"

"They were outside hustlin' when I was in the pool so I know they got a little bread on them." Jr. said.

193

Prince and the nigga at table looked at each other. They had heard there were some bad bitches hustling and making every dime that came through. Once Babygurl saw them look at each other, she knew what time it was. Ole boy came from under the table with a nine pointed at them.

"Since y'all getting money, how about your fine asses, come off of whatever y'all go on y'all."

"Nigga, you got us for fu——"

"Bitch, just give it to them."

Babygurl, being with the Stick Up squad, knew to give up what they could get back, plus she knew they weren't killas. Jr. walked to them and relieved Babygurl for a zone, some loose rocks, and $600. Prince got something from Keisha, but she had $800.

"You are getting a li'l money for real, huh?" said Prince

"We gonna sample that pussy, but we're gonna let y'all make it."

When he said that, Keisha spit in his face and he slapped blood from her mouth.

"Chill, Jr. Y'all get up out of here before something happens to y'all that we might regret."

Keisha was the first one out of the door, holding her face. Babygurl looked back one more time and took off at a fast pace to their spot. She was so mad that she was red. Keisha saw it in her eyes and knew what was about to happen. She went and grabbed two nines, handed one to Keisha, then left back out. Keisha didn't ask questions because Babygurl was her friend. Everybody was looking at them because their straps was out. When they made it to the door, they heard them laughing about what just happened. Once Babygurl knocked, they answered without knowing who it was.

"What the fuck? These bitches——"

194

Grimey Ways

That was all he said before Keisha put a bullet in his head and he fell face first. Babygurl walked in and shot three times before Prince fell backwards. When they got to where ole boy was crouched behind the couch, Babygurl and Keisha walked up on him

"You picked the wrong bitches to jack, bitch-ass nigga!" said Babygurl as they emptied the whole clip in his body.

They grabbed everything they could and left without leaving a soul or fingerprint.

Ray Vinci

Chapter 31

It had been three days since Correy had told him about Rico and he was finally bringing it up to his squad. Everybody was there including the few he put on. Altogether there were fifteen of them.

"Alright, remember when I came home and we did that lick on Rico?" asked Kilo.

"Yeah, so what about it?" Slugga asked, confused

"Well, Correy asked me to find the niggas that killed his best friend, which was Rico. The only thing he remembers is you." He pointed at Babygurl.

"That's where I've seen that nigga at. The day we popped off Rico, he was the nigga he copped the bricks from, and he was the one following me that day," she said, looking shocked.

Mr. Lee wasn't surprised because all Correy was talking about in jail was getting the niggas who did it, but he didn't know it was Kilo. Kilo explained that they were gon' hold out for a little while until Correy made his move because he was pretty sure Correy knew it was them. Some of them didn't like the fact that they were losing a big source of their money, but they weren't tripping.

"I know what y'all thinking. I've been preparing, so Mr. Lee contacted some of his people he used to work with, and we got a new plug. Just when push comes to shove, we gonna have to keep what's ours and take what's his," Kilo explained.

"Let's just go air the nigga out right now before shit get out of hand," said Felony.

"Naw, let's play our cards right and will win the game," he shot back.

Mr. Lee just nodded his head because Kilo was listening and becoming the boss he was meant to be.

***

Corey, Philly, Tidy, Quick, Keisha, Tre, and the rest of his people were at his spot in the Landings. He had everybody there because he wanted to inform them about his situation with Kilo and his squad.

"We got a situation on our hands that's not gon' end pretty," Correy said, lighting up a Newport.

"What's up, yo? Talk to us," said Philly.

"Alright, remember when my homeboy Rico got killed? Well, I've been trying to find out who did it. All I know is that he was last seen with a Mexican, which is Babygurl!"

The first person that was shocked by the name was Keisha. She and Babygurl were close, so she didn't know what to think.

"I started putting shit together and the five bricks that I bought from Kilo was the same ones Rico copped from me that day he got killed. I've seen Babygurl in action and I know she gangsta enough to do it. I don't know if Kilo got anything to do with it, but that's his girl, so I know it's gonna be some trouble on that end," Correy said.

Everybody was fucked up about what was happening because Kilo and his crew were one of the main reasons they were attacked. They didn't wanna lose a good squad, but Correy was out for revenge for Rico.

"Shit, it's whateva, gangsta, you know we gon' ride!" said Quick while showing both his guns.

"I got a feeling you ain't done explaining," said Tre.

"I'm not. Me knowing Kilo, he not gonna want to give up his spots, so we just let him keep them and protect ours in the process."

Correy was smart so he didn't want to trip over no bullshit, but if it was Kilo and his squad that killed Rico, he was gonna make sure everyone on his team was gon' die for it.

As soon as he walked away from the table, his phone rang. When he saw it was Kilo, he picked up.

"What up?"

"What up, gangsta, where are you at? I need a couple of them thangs from you," said Kilo.

"Okay, meet me at Deerwood later on tonight. Oh, and I need to chop it up with you on some G shit."

"Alright, I got to handle some business, then me and Baby-gurl gonna slide through."

"That's a bet."

Correy walked back into the house and Keisha was sitting by herself. She looked at him and rolled her eyes. She was probably mad because of the way he left her after he had fucked. He had been meaning to talk to her about them niggas she and Babygurl had shot and killed, but that could wait.

Everybody else was in the living room playing the game and smoking, so he went straight to the back. When he came back, Keisha was gone. He wasn't feeling the way she was acting, but let it go. He told his crew he was about to meet up with Kilo, so Quick dipped with him.

***

Babygurl had pulled up in front of the apartment Kilo had in Oak Manor to pick him up. She had bought a white-on-white Audi and knew she looked good in it. She blew the horn

199

Ray Vinci

and Kilo came out with one blunt lit and two behind his ear. When he got in the car, he kissed her and then she drove off. She turned up her Nicki Minaj, then reached for the Sweet Kilo was smoking.

"So what's up, what you about to cop?" she asked.

"About three. Shit been slow lately."

"It's jumping in Deerwood. You can trap over there for a few days."

"Naw, I'm good, plus I might end up laying that dick on Keisha," he said while eyeing Babygurl.

"Don't get you or her smoked! Bad enough I got to share that bitch with Lexi."

"Damn, I'm just playing, girl," he said while laughing. He knew she was for real. "I heard about them niggas you and Keisha smoked the other day. Why didn't you let me handle it?"

"Because, that nigga tried to play us in our own spot. We can't let shit like that happen."

"I didn't know Keisha had it in her, to be honest with you," he said.

"What do you expect when you fucking with a gangsta bitch?"

Kilo lit another blunt as they pulled up to Babygurl's trap. She turned down the music and then got out. Kilo stayed in the car for a couple of minutes and then took the key out and walked inside. When he walked in, Babygurl and Keisha was talking and laughing so he went straight to the back where Correy and Quick were.

"What's good, gangstas?" he said to both of them.

"Nothing, just waiting on you," said Correy.

Kilo passed him the Sweet he was smoking then leaned up against the door as Babygurl came in and gave Correy some

200

money for a brick. She left and went right back talking to Keisha.

"Bitch, I got to talk to you about some shit. I need you to tell me something and keep it 100," he said with a serious look.

"Shoot," she replied.

"Correy just told us about his homeboy Rico and he said you and your boys had something to do with it."

The whole time Keisha was talking, Babygurl replayed the whole scene in her head so she could remember every detail. She was also replaying the conversation Kilo was having with the squad and him thinking that Correy knew. Now that Keisha was asking her about it, it confirmed that he knew. She was so caught up in her thoughts that she didn't hear Correy come out or see him standing in the hallway.

"Look, bitch, it was a thing me and my squad used to do, so I'ma keep it real with you. Yeah, we did it, but we didn't know shit like this was gonna happen, and we sure didn't know nothing about Correy."

As she explained, Correy got mad because he knew she had something to do with it, but he didn't like the fact that Kilo did as well. He pulled his strap out before he even knew he did it and stepped around the corner with it pointed to the back of her head.

"Bitch, I knew it was you! I knew it from the first time you walked through the door that you set my nigga up!"

He was so mad and caught up in his words that he didn't see Babygurl pull out her nine and point it at him.

"We didn't know shit was gonna go down like this."

"Fuck! What! You! Knew! Or! Didn't! Know!" Correy yelled.

Quick and Kilo heard the yelling and ran to the living room. Quick made it there before Kilo. When he saw the straps, he pulled his, then pointed it at Babygurl. Kilo saw them pointing straps at Babygurl and pulled his on Quick.

"Look, everybody calm down before some shit happens that we don't want," Kilo said, clenching his teeth.

"Fuck that! Somebody gotta die for my nigga!"

Keisha was so confused. She looked from Babygurl to Quick to Correy. She was getting money with them both, but Babygurl was her girl, so she pulled her strap and pointed it at Correy.

"Babygurl, Kilo, let's get out of here!" she said.

Every last one of them was confused, but Correy was outnumbered so he let them go.

Grimey Ways

Ray Vinci

Chapter 32

Kilo, Babygurl, and Keisha sped off in Babygurl's Audi with the music turned down. They rode in silence for a while, and the only reason Keisha said something was because they were both staring at her through the mirrors.

"So, what happens from here, because I just turned my back on the niggas who looked out for me?" she said with her head down.

It was still quiet for a while before Kilo said something. "Don't worry about it. You can fuck with us from now on. But I gotta know if your loyalty is with us before this shit jumps off?" asked Kilo.

"My loyalty is with Babygurl, and if she fuck with y'all, then my loyalty is with y'all."

That was the answer he wanted to hear. He lit up a Newport and then dialed Illy's number.

"What's up, big bro? Talk to me."

"Meet me at the spot and make sure everybody there."

It took twenty minutes to get to the east side and when they got there, the whole squad was waiting on them.

"What's up, gangsta, what's going on" asked Slugga.

"I'll explain it when we get inside."

They walked in the house and Kilo went straight to his room and packed up all his money and the bricks he had stashed in two duffel bags. He put them in Babygurl's Audi, then walked back in.

"Alright, Correy found out about Rico and pulled his banger out on Babygurl. We all had our straps out and Keisha had the drop on Correy, so he let us go." He explained everything that went down with the help of Babygurl and Keisha adding their input.

So, you telling me didn't nobody bust they straps?" Lowkey asked.

"Naw, but somebody about to die behind this shit!" said Babygurl.

"So, what's about to happen?" asked Felony.

"We keep the spots we got and take his in the process. Whoever gets in the way, let them have it, because as far as I'm concerned, we run this shit," said Kilo

"I can help," Keisha said as everybody looked at her. "I know he keeps all his money and work in the room in Deerwood. If we hit the spot, we just might hurt him a little bit."

Everybody was nodding their heads because it was a good idea.

"Alright, that's our first move and we do that tonight," said Kilo.

***

"I can't believe this bitch had the nerve to ride with that bitch-ass nigga and pull a heat on me!" said Correy as he weaved through the traffic.

"She gonna be the first one I smoke," was all Quick could say because he couldn't believe she had done some shit like that.

Correy made it to Springhill and parked his truck in front of the apartment. When he walked in, he saw Lovey, Lexi, and Lisa sitting on the couch smoking and playing with the baby. He looked at Lexi and Lisa and all he saw was Kilo and Slugga. Quick walked in and he saw the same thing.

"What's wrong with y'all?" Lovey asked Quick.

He didn't answer. He just followed Correy. When he walked in the bedroom, Correy was talking on the phone and bagging up the few straps he had there.

"I told Tre to meet us at Landing's apartments tonight and bring the crew."

"Alright."

They walked back up front and noticed it was quiet before they walked out the door. He turned towards Lisa and Lexi.

"Tell y'all niggas they dead," he said, then slammed the door.

They jumped back in his ride and smashed off towards the landings. He thought about how shit was about to go down and didn't like the situation he was left in. He had seen Kilo and his squad in action and knew they were going to be tough to handle. He was nervous, so he kept checking his rearview every time mirror.

"I know they gon' shut down their spots, so we need to find a different way to get out them," said Quick.

"I know. I'm trying to see how we gon' do that. Just know whatever goes down, it won't be easy."

"I can't believe that bad-ass bitch did some shit like that. And to think I was about to try it there. Damn, that bitch dangerous."

"I'm gonna make that bitch suffer, so she better be ready."

The rest of the way was quiet because they were both deep in thought. When they pulled up to the landings, they were both alert because Kilo was smart and dangerous, so they didn't take any chances.

Once they saw it was good, they pulled in front of their spot. They had a little time to kill before everybody got there, so they lit up some blunts then came up with the plan of their own.

Ray Vinci

Chapter 33

"I'm gonna be through tomorrow to drop some money off that I need you to put up," he said to Bianca.

"What's going on? Why do you sound anxious?" she asked.

"It's nothing. Let me call you back. I got to take this call on the other end."

"Okay, be careful and I'll see you tomorrow," she said and then hung up.

He clicked over. Lexi's voice was shaky as she talked.

"What's going on, baby? Correy just left here with guns and told me to tell y'all. What happened?" asked Lexi.

"Some shit went down with his homie that died and we had something to do with it. And now all the shit came back to us. Look, go home and don't talk to nobody and I'll talk to you later."

"Okay, but make sure you come home."

"I got to make sure I handle my business first."

She didn't know if Correy's threat was serious, but she knew Kilo's words.

"Okay, just be careful. We need you."

"I will, half-breed. I love you," he said, then hung up.

After he hung up, everybody was ready to go. It was like old times with him and his squad, but this time they had Mr. Lee and Keisha with them.

"Okay, once we get everything, we get out. If there's anybody there, we make sure they're not breathing before we leave."

"When we get in, everything is stashed in the room with the lock on it. Most of his money is there, and all of his work is there for sure."

"How do you know this?" Illy asked.

"Because I saw it in his closet three days ago," she shot back.

"Cool. Let's roll out."

Babygurl rode with Kilo with Keisha in the backseat. He turned up his music and then smashed off. Babygurl and Keisha were checking their straps just in case somebody was inside.

It took them twenty minutes to get there. They drove around, making sure nobody was outside watching them. He didn't want to tell his squad, but he felt like Keisha was setting them up. If she was, he planned on smoking her on sight. Once he was satisfied nobody was watching, he parked his truck and stepped out.

He started walking towards the apartment with his squad right behind him. He checked the knob to see if it was locked and when he found that it was, Keisha tried her key. When that didn't work, he knew they changed the locks.

"Watch out. Step to the side," Kilo said to Keisha.

Before she could even get out of the way, Kilo kicked the door and the whole squad went in without thinking twice. They all had their guns pointed in front of them as Keisha and Babygurl let them to the room where everything was at. Keisha shot at the lock and everybody ducked out of the way, not wanting to get hit by the bullet.

"Get everything, and don't leave nothing behind," said Kilo.

Babygurl turned on the lights as Kilo and Keisha went to open the closet. Once they opened it, the smell of coke hit their

210

nose. He saw at least twenty-five bricks and three duffel bags full of money. They grabbed the three duffel bags and threw them outside to Slugga. They found some empty bags and stuffed the bricks in. What they couldn't fit, they carried by hand. They loaded up everything and drove off.

***

Correy, Quick, and Tre sat a couple of houses down from Kilo's, making sure nobody was there. They didn't see any movement, so they jumped out and jogged to the house. Tre check the door and it opened. Once they noticed it wasn't locked, they pulled their bangas out and pointed them towards the door.

"Take everything that looks like dope and money," Correy said.

They tore the house up and couldn't find anything.

"Fuck!" Correy yelled. Kilo had outsmarted him.

Kilo had moved everything out before he left just in case Correy was planning on doing the same thing they were doing.

"Come on, let's go He got smart and moved everything. We're gonna have to find another way. If not, whenever I see any one of them they are dead," he said as he walked out the door.

They jogged back to their rides and smashed up towards Deerwood.

***

The squad had split up the money and bricks they had hit Correy for last night, so they were good to shut down all the spots for a couple of days.

"Good morning, baby, you sleep well?" Bianca asked Kilo.

He had forgotten he had come to the house last night. She gave him a kiss, then got up.

"Yeah, I did. How about you?"

Before she could answer, his phone rang. When he saw it was Correy, he laughed and then answered it.

"I guess I outsmarted you because I got everything and you assed out," Kilo said.

"Fuck you, bitch-ass nigga! When I see you, you dead, pussy!"

"Yeah, whateva. Just make sure you strapped all the time and watch your back, because I'm coming. Oh yeah! And your spots too," he said and then hung up

He laid down and plotted on multiple ways to get at Correy.

To be continued...
Grimy Wayz II
Gangstas, Hustlers, and Savages

Grimey Ways

Lock Down Publications and Ca$h Presents assisted publishing packages.

BASIC PACKAGE $499
Editing
Cover Design
Formatting

UPGRADED PACKAGE $800
Typing
Editing
Cover Design
Formatting

ADVANCE PACKAGE $1,200
Typing
Editing
Cover Design
Formatting
Copyright registration
Proofreading
Upload book to Amazon

LDP SUPREME PACKAGE $1,500
Typing
Editing
Cover Design
Formatting
Copyright registration
Proofreading
Set up Amazon account

Ray Vinci

Upload book to Amazon
Advertise on LDP Amazon and Facebook page

***Other services available upon request. Additional charges may apply
Lock Down Publications
P.O. Box 944
Stockbridge, GA 30281-9998
Phone # 470 303-9761

Submission Guideline

Submit the first three chapters of your completed manuscript to ldpsubmissions@gmail.com, subject line: Your book's title. The manuscript must be in a .doc file and sent as an attachment. Document should be in Times New Roman, double spaced and in size 12 font. Also, provide your synopsis and full contact information. If sending multiple submissions, they must each be in a separate email.

Have a story but no way to send it electronically? You can still submit to LDP/Ca$h Presents. Send in the first three chapters, written or typed, of your completed manuscript to:

LDP: Submissions Dept
Po Box 944
Stockbridge, Ga 30281

DO NOT send original manuscript. Must be a duplicate.

Provide your synopsis and a cover letter containing your full contact information.

Thanks for considering LDP and Ca$h Presents.

NEW RELEASES

MONEY IN THE GRAVE 2 by MARTELL
"TROUBLESOME" BOLDEN
THE BRICK MAN 2 by KING RIO
A DOPEBOY'S DREAM 3 by ROMELL
TUKES
CONFESSIONS OF A JACKBOY II by
NICHOLAS LOCK
A GANGSTA'S KARMA 2 by FLAME
GRIMEY WAYS by RAY VINCI

BLOOD OF A BOSS **VI**

SHADOWS OF THE GAME II

TRAP BASTARD II

By **Askari**

LOYAL TO THE GAME **IV**

By **T.J. & Jelissa**

IF TRUE SAVAGE **VIII**

MIDNIGHT CARTEL IV

DOPE BOY MAGIC IV

CITY OF KINGZ III

NIGHTMARE ON SILENT AVE II

By **Chris Green**

BLAST FOR ME **III**

A SAVAGE DOPEBOY III

CUTTHROAT MAFIA III

DUFFLE BAG CARTEL VII

HEARTLESS GOON VI

By **Ghost**

A HUSTLER'S DECEIT III

KILL ZONE II

BAE BELONGS TO ME III

By **Aryanna**

KING OF THE TRAP III

By **T.J. Edwards**

GORILLAZ IN THE BAY V

Ray Vinci

3X KRAZY III

STRAIGHT BEAST MODE II

De'Kari

KINGPIN KILLAZ IV

STREET KINGS III

PAID IN BLOOD III

CARTEL KILLAZ IV

DOPE GODS III

Hood Rich

SINS OF A HUSTLA II

ASAD

RICH $AVAGE II

MONEY IN THE GRAVE II

By Martell Troublesome Bolden

YAYO V

Bred In The Game 2

S. Allen

CREAM III

By Yolanda Moore

SON OF A DOPE FIEND III

HEAVEN GOT A GHETTO II

By Renta

LOYALTY AIN'T PROMISED III

By Keith Williams

I'M NOTHING WITHOUT HIS LOVE II

SINS OF A THUG II

Grimey Ways

TO THE THUG I LOVED BEFORE II

By Monet Dragun

QUIET MONEY IV

EXTENDED CLIP III

THUG LIFE IV

By **Trai'Quan**

THE STREETS MADE ME IV

By **Larry D. Wright**

IF YOU CROSS ME ONCE II

By **Anthony Fields**

THE STREETS WILL NEVER CLOSE II

By K'ajji

HARD AND RUTHLESS III

THE BILLIONAIRE BENTLEYS II

Von Diesel

KILLA KOUNTY II

By Khufu

MONEY GAME III

By Smoove Dolla

JACK BOYZ VERSUS DOPE BOYZ

By Romell Tukes

MURDA WAS THE CASE II

Elijah R. Freeman

THE STREETS NEVER LET GO II

By Robert Baptiste

AN UNFORESEEN LOVE III

Ray Vinci

By **Meesha**

KING OF THE TRENCHES II

by **GHOST & TRANAY ADAMS**

MONEY MAFIA II

LOYAL TO THE SOIL II

By **Jibril Williams**

QUEEN OF THE ZOO II

By **Black Migo**

THE BRICK MAN III

By King Rio

VICIOUS LOYALTY II

By Kingpen

A GANGSTA'S PAIN II

By J-Blunt

CONFESSIONS OF A JACKBOY III

By Nicholas Lock

GRIMEY WAYS II

By Ray Vinci

Grimey Ways

Available Now

RESTRAINING ORDER **I & II**

By **CA$H & Coffee**

LOVE KNOWS NO BOUNDARIES **I II & III**

By **Coffee**

RAISED AS A GOON I, II, III & IV

BRED BY THE SLUMS I, II, III

BLAST FOR ME I & II

ROTTEN TO THE CORE I II III

A BRONX TALE I, II, III

DUFFLE BAG CARTEL I II III IV V VI

HEARTLESS GOON I II III IV V

A SAVAGE DOPEBOY I II

DRUG LORDS I II III

CUTTHROAT MAFIA I II

KING OF THE TRENCHES

By **Ghost**

LAY IT DOWN **I & II**

LAST OF A DYING BREED I II

BLOOD STAINS OF A SHOTTA I & II III

By **Jamaica**

LOYAL TO THE GAME I II III

LIFE OF SIN I, II III

By **TJ & Jelissa**

221

Ray Vinci

BLOODY COMMAS I & II

SKI MASK CARTEL I II & III

KING OF NEW YORK I II,III IV V

RISE TO POWER I II III

COKE KINGS I II III IV V

BORN HEARTLESS I II III IV

KING OF THE TRAP I II

By **T.J. Edwards**

IF LOVING HIM IS WRONG…I & II

LOVE ME EVEN WHEN IT HURTS I II III

By **Jelissa**

WHEN THE STREETS CLAP BACK I & II III

THE HEART OF A SAVAGE I II III

MONEY MAFIA

LOYAL TO THE SOIL

By **Jibril Williams**

A DISTINGUISHED THUG STOLE MY HEART I II & III

LOVE SHOULDN'T HURT I II III IV

RENEGADE BOYS I II III IV

PAID IN KARMA I II III

SAVAGE STORMS I II

AN UNFORESEEN LOVE I II

By **Meesha**

A GANGSTER'S CODE I &, II III

A GANGSTER'S SYN I II III

THE SAVAGE LIFE I II III

222

Grimey Ways

CHAINED TO THE STREETS I II III

BLOOD ON THE MONEY I II III

A GANGSTA'S PAIN

By J-Blunt

PUSH IT TO THE LIMIT

By **Bre' Hayes**

BLOOD OF A BOSS **I, II, III, IV, V**

SHADOWS OF THE GAME

TRAP BASTARD

By **Askari**

THE STREETS BLEED MURDER **I, II & III**

THE HEART OF A GANGSTA I II& III

By **Jerry Jackson**

CUM FOR ME I II III IV V VI VII

An **LDP Erotica Collaboration**

BRIDE OF A HUSTLA **I II & II**

THE FETTI GIRLS **I, II& III**

CORRUPTED BY A GANGSTA I, II III, IV

BLINDED BY HIS LOVE

THE PRICE YOU PAY FOR LOVE I, II ,III

DOPE GIRL MAGIC I II III

By **Destiny Skai**

WHEN A GOOD GIRL GOES BAD

By **Adrienne**

THE COST OF LOYALTY I II III

By Kweli

Ray Vinci

A GANGSTER'S REVENGE **I II III & IV**

THE BOSS MAN'S DAUGHTERS I II III IV V

A SAVAGE LOVE **I & II**

BAE BELONGS TO ME I II

A HUSTLER'S DECEIT I, II, III

WHAT BAD BITCHES DO I, II, III

SOUL OF A MONSTER I II III

KILL ZONE

A DOPE BOY'S QUEEN I II III

By **Aryanna**

A KINGPIN'S AMBITON

A KINGPIN'S AMBITION **II**

I MURDER FOR THE DOUGH

By **Ambitious**

TRUE SAVAGE I II III IV V VI VII

DOPE BOY MAGIC I, II, III

MIDNIGHT CARTEL I II III

CITY OF KINGZ I II

NIGHTMARE ON SILENT AVE

By **Chris Green**

A DOPEBOY'S PRAYER

By **Eddie "Wolf" Lee**

THE KING CARTEL **I, II & III**

By **Frank Gresham**

THESE NIGGAS AIN'T LOYAL **I, II & III**

By **Nikki Tee**

Grimey Ways

GANGSTA SHYT **I II &III**

By **CATO**

THE ULTIMATE BETRAYAL

By **Phoenix**

BOSS'N UP **I , II & III**

By **Royal Nicole**

I LOVE YOU TO DEATH

By **Destiny J**

I RIDE FOR MY HITTA

I STILL RIDE FOR MY HITTA

By **Misty Holt**

LOVE & CHASIN' PAPER

By **Qay Crockett**

TO DIE IN VAIN

SINS OF A HUSTLA

By **ASAD**

BROOKLYN HUSTLAZ

By **Boogsy Morina**

BROOKLYN ON LOCK I & II

By **Sonovia**

GANGSTA CITY

By **Teddy Duke**

A DRUG KING AND HIS DIAMOND I & II III

A DOPEMAN'S RICHES

HER MAN, MINE'S TOO I, II

CASH MONEY HO'S

225

Ray Vinci

THE WIFEY I USED TO BE I II
By Nicole Goosby
TRAPHOUSE KING **I II & III**
KINGPIN KILLAZ I II III
STREET KINGS I II
PAID IN BLOOD **I II**
CARTEL KILLAZ I II III
DOPE GODS I II
By **Hood Rich**
LIPSTICK KILLAH **I, II, III**
CRIME OF PASSION I II & III
FRIEND OR FOE I II III
By **Mimi**
STEADY MOBBN' **I, II, III**
THE STREETS STAINED MY SOUL I II
By **Marcellus Allen**
WHO SHOT YA **I, II, III**
SON OF A DOPE FIEND I II
HEAVEN GOT A GHETTO
Renta
GORILLAZ IN THE BAY **I II III IV**
TEARS OF A GANGSTA I II
3X KRAZY I II
STRAIGHT BEAST MODE
DE'KARI
TRIGGADALE I II III

226

Grimey Ways

MURDAROBER WAS THE CASE

Elijah R. Freeman

GOD BLESS THE TRAPPERS I, II, III

THESE SCANDALOUS STREETS I, II, III

FEAR MY GANGSTA I, II, III IV, V

THESE STREETS DON'T LOVE NOBODY I, II

BURY ME A G I, II, III, IV, V

A GANGSTA'S EMPIRE I, II, III, IV

THE DOPEMAN'S BODYGAURD I II

THE REALEST KILLAZ I II III

THE LAST OF THE OGS I II III

Tranay Adams

THE STREETS ARE CALLING

Duquie Wilson

MARRIED TO A BOSS I II III

By Destiny Skai & Chris Green

KINGZ OF THE GAME I II III IV V VI

Playa Ray

SLAUGHTER GANG I II III

RUTHLESS HEART I II III

By Willie Slaughter

FUK SHYT

By Blakk Diamond

DON'T F#CK WITH MY HEART I II

By Linnea

ADDICTED TO THE DRAMA I II III

Ray Vinci

IN THE ARM OF HIS BOSS II

By Jamila

YAYO I II III IV

A SHOOTER'S AMBITION I II

BRED IN THE GAME

By S. Allen

TRAP GOD I II III

RICH $AVAGE

MONEY IN THE GRAVE I II

By Martell Troublesome Bolden

FOREVER GANGSTA

GLOCKS ON SATIN SHEETS I II

By Adrian Dulan

TOE TAGZ I II III

LEVELS TO THIS SHYT I II

By Ah'Million

KINGPIN DREAMS I II III

By Paper Boi Rari

CONFESSIONS OF A GANGSTA I II III IV

CONFESSIONS OF A JACKBOY I II

By Nicholas Lock

I'M NOTHING WITHOUT HIS LOVE

SINS OF A THUG

TO THE THUG I LOVED BEFORE

By Monet Dragun

CAUGHT UP IN THE LIFE I II III

228

Grimey Ways

THE STREETS NEVER LET GO
By Robert Baptiste
NEW TO THE GAME I II III
MONEY, MURDER & MEMORIES I II III
By **Malik D. Rice**
LIFE OF A SAVAGE I II III
A GANGSTA'S QUR'AN I II III
MURDA SEASON I II III
GANGLAND CARTEL I II III
CHI'RAQ GANGSTAS I II III
KILLERS ON ELM STREET I II III
JACK BOYZ N DA BRONX I II III
A DOPEBOY'S DREAM I II III
By **Romell Tukes**
LOYALTY AIN'T PROMISED I II
By Keith Williams
QUIET MONEY I II III
THUG LIFE I II III
EXTENDED CLIP I II
By **Trai'Quan**
THE STREETS MADE ME I II III
By **Larry D. Wright**
THE ULTIMATE SACRIFICE I, II, III, IV, V, VI
KHADIFI
IF YOU CROSS ME ONCE
ANGEL I II

229

Ray Vinci

IN THE BLINK OF AN EYE
By **Anthony Fields**
THE LIFE OF A HOOD STAR
By Ca$h & Rashia Wilson
THE STREETS WILL NEVER CLOSE
By K'ajji
CREAM I II
By Yolanda Moore
NIGHTMARES OF A HUSTLA I II III
By King Dream
CONCRETE KILLA I II
VICIOUS LOYALTY
By Kingpen
HARD AND RUTHLESS I II
MOB TOWN 251
THE BILLIONAIRE BENTLEYS
By Von Diesel
GHOST MOB
Stilloan Robinson
MOB TIES I II III IV
By SayNoMore
BODYMORE MURDERLAND I II III
By Delmont Player
FOR THE LOVE OF A BOSS
By C. D. Blue
MOBBED UP I II III IV

Grimey Ways

THE BRICK MAN I II
By King Rio
KILLA KOUNTY
By Khufu
MONEY GAME I II
By Smoove Dolla
A GANGSTA'S KARMA I II
By FLAME
KING OF THE TRENCHES II
by **GHOST & TRANAY ADAMS**
QUEEN OF THE ZOO
By **Black Migo**
GRIMEY WAYS
By Ray Vinci

Ray Vinci

BOOKS BY LDP'S CEO, CA$H

TRUST IN NO MAN

TRUST IN NO MAN 2

TRUST IN NO MAN 3

BONDED BY BLOOD

SHORTY GOT A THUG

THUGS CRY

THUGS CRY 2

THUGS CRY 3

TRUST NO BITCH

TRUST NO BITCH 2

TRUST NO BITCH 3

TIL MY CASKET DROPS

RESTRAINING ORDER

RESTRAINING ORDER 2

IN LOVE WITH A CONVICT

LIFE OF A HOOD STAR

Grimey Ways

9 781955 270755